COLD DEADLY STARE . . .

Nick let the full effect of his stare settle before striding purposefully over to the table and leaning over the German. There were two very definitive sounds that accompanied the action. One, Nick's fist slamming onto the table in front of the man. Two, Wilhelmina, Nick's gun, slamming down to his right.

Nick's voice, when it came, was arctic. "Let me be blunt. I may be new, but only to you. I've been running missions for more years than I care to recall, and I'm still alive to tell about it. Which is more than I can say for most of the people who have tried to cross me . . ."

NICK CARTER IS IT!

FROM THE NICK CARTER
KILLMASTER SERIES

NICK CARTER

KILLMASTER

THE DEATH DEALER

CHARTER BOOKS, NEW YORK

THE DEATH DEALER

A Charter Book/published by arrangement with
The Condé Nast Publications, Inc.

PRINTING HISTORY
Charter Original/August 1983

ISBN: 0-441-14217-6

Charter Books are published by The Berkley Publishing Group,
200 Madison Avenue, New York, New York 10016.
PRINTED IN THE UNITED STATES OF AMERICA

*Dedicated to the men of the
Secret Services of the
United States of America*

PROLOGUE

WINTER 1970

BERLIN

The muscles in Nick's neck tensed, relaxed, and then almost immediately tensed again. It had been the same for the last hour.

The deal stunk. His tempered senses, every instinct, told him so. And the grinning face of Jacobi, the German, sitting across the table from him didn't alleviate the feeling. Too hard, Nick slammed his cup on the table. He ignored the coffee that leapt out to dot the tabletop. Heaving himself to his feet with an audible groan, he stalked like a caged cat to the window. Purposely, he remained oblivious as Jacobi withdrew a spotless handkerchief from his inside pocket and meticulously blotted up the coffee. In seconds the tabletop was returned to its original pristine squalor.

"You are restive, Herr Mercury." Jacobi's whiny

voice all but chuckled. Following his words came a short burst of "tsk, tsks" that only served to tighten the muscles in Nick's neck. "We have been running our little underground railroad for many years now. We are good at what we do."

Yeah, Nick thought, and what you do and who you do it for is what's worrying me.

Nick acknowledged the fat man's words with silence as his eyes floated out the window and down.

Several floors below him was roughly seventy yards of earth—a fraction so small, in global terms, that it defied calculation. And yet he might as well be staring at another galaxy.

At his feet were fifteen yards of sidewalk and street, bordered by a high wooden fence. Beyond that, fifteen more yards of patrolled road, and a second wire fence. Farther on, Nick's eye picked out a perimeter of tank traps created by crosses of lumber, weirdly tilted. Beyond that, thirty more yards of mine field that culminated in a concrete wall that fully underscored the subtlety of the Slavic mind.

Across this labyrinth, the flickering lights of West Berlin; within, the Minotaur of the Soviet presence.

And over it all hung the pall of a gathering fog. Like ghostly gray fingers it seemed to seep up from the concrete to partially obscure everything it touched. Even objects already in shadow seemed to get darker and take on grotesque shapes.

"The fog is rolling in . . . heavier," Nick said, more to himself than to the man behind him.

"All the better for our purpose," came the reply.

All in all, he thought, not the best position for an undercover AXE operative like Nick Carter, who liked to pick his own ground for battle.

Nick turned from the window and stared at his companion. He was an ill-kempt slob of a man, grown fat from bartering human lives. Jacobi returned his look with a wink and a quick thumbs-up. Nick's gaze dropped to the table.

"You missed a spot," he said, and watched with distaste as the man again produced his handkerchief and snatched up one last hint of coffee stain from the oaken top of the table.

"Can't be too careful," Jacobi chirped.

That's obvious, thought Nick as he turned back to the window.

Out there somewhere was a man Nick knew only as the Dealer, a man who, for a price, ferried live bodies from East to West—sometimes. The Dealer was an enigma, a man without a face, without a name.

Nick Carter didn't like enigmas.

It was said that the Dealer could work either side of the wall, and that was why he kept his identity so secret, his presence so much in the shadows.

Nick didn't like, or trust, what he couldn't see.

He rolled his cuff up and flicked his eyes down to the dial on his special issue AXE watch. "They're late."

"Patience, Herr Mercury, patience."

Patience, bullshit, Nick thought, knowing the fog would help this night's defection, but wishing his eyes could penetrate it.

The truck hit a bump in the road, tossing its occupants like cucumbers in a salad. Four bodies lifted and dropped again amid the cacophony of squawking chickens. Each, in his own section of the flatbed, struggled to keep his shielding of piled-up coops from toppling. The truck punctuated the event by backfiring, and then lumbered on, its equilibrium once more intact.

The engine echoed back down the narrow street, the internal explosions doing little to settle the nerves of its occupants. The railroad was running late, but still *running*. That counted for something.

Jacek, the appointed leader of the fleeing quartet, gave

a quick check of the rigging supporting the surrounding coops. Tenuous, came the verdict, but still holding. His head then craned to the left, his eyes searching through planes of wire and meandering feathers to find the only other member of the four he could see.

Stefan responded to the feel of Jacek's eyes, returning the look with a quick darting of tongue over lips before breaking out in a wide, gleaming grin that said much more for his youthful bravado than it ever did of his courage. The voice that followed was wobbly, but optimistic.

"Making up time, eh, Jacek? Mercury will wait, no? Tomorrow, my friend. You'll see. Beer in the Tiergarten. Liters of it, yes?"

Jacek's face broke out in a smile. The boy's energy was too contagious to ignore. "Liters, my young friend," he nodded. "And women, Stefan. Big women. Women for your canvases, and women for your bed."

The boy's head bobbed excitedly, and his smile grew impossibly wider. His head then dropped away, arms resting behind him, as his eyes began creating feminine forms in the inky blackness of the sky above. Jacek watched him a few seconds more before relaxing his own head.

There was only a mere ten years between their ages, but Jacek felt more like father than brother to the boy. Shared nationality, and seven years of living and fighting beneath the Communist fist, made for odd friendships. The truck's other two refugees were indisputably brilliant and dedicated men, scientists both, but they held little of Jacek's interest. Their fate was of no concern.

But Stefan was different. He was young and rash, a dreamer of the worst kind. He was a painter of enormous talent, and a terminal idealist. Jacek knew the world would eventually chew him up and spit him out, and it evoked in him a kind of pity—a kind of love.

Jacek settled back, pausing only to steal a quick glance at his watch. In minutes they would make their rendezvous. There was a brief surge of excitement in his belly, and then, just as quickly, it passed. The Dealer was in charge. By definition, everything was under control.

No, thought Jacek, the scientists are of no concern. Their fates are sealed. The Dealer has called for their deaths, and countermanding that order would be inconceivable. But Stefan shall live. The Dealer has promised it. It shall be my one consolation in the years of work ahead.

For now, let the boy have his dreams.

Nick gave a start as a loud crack pierced the night air. His eyes flew down to the base of the wall where the accompanying flash had sparked. Just as quickly his muscles relaxed. The single spark became many, and the crack evolved into a staccato burst of firecrackers. From the Western side of the wall came a defiant yell of childish voices, then laughter, then the scurrying of youthful feet.

Today's pranksters—tomorrow's political giants. Would any of them ever see this hideous line of concrete torn down? Questions, thought Nick, that are not mine to answer. I'm the action man, the liaison on the scene to make sure that, this time, the Dealer delivers *all* the bodies he's been contracted for.

"We're not sure of this Dealer," David Hawk, head of AXE, had said. "But right now he's all we have. Be there, N3—and watch yourself."

As if in response to the thought, Nick's hand slipped beneath the leather exterior of his jacket. He pulled out Wilhelmina, enjoying the cool comfort of the Luger's steel body in his hands, the crisp sound of its mechanics as the clip slid out to display its readiness. Satisfied, he slid the clip home and levered a shell into the chamber.

The action did not go unnoticed.

"Relax, my friend," Jacobi muttered. "These things take time. You cannot run on schedules, *ja?* The Dealer knows his business. You will see. You are new. You will learn."

Nick turned and flashed the fat man an icy glare. There was a second or two of shrugging, smiling, even a wave of the hand, as though the German could clear the stink of danger from the air with a mere gesture. But after all the antics, the reality of Nick's stare began to reach him. There was a kind of peeling back of the skin, a reaching into the man with eyes so cold they burned.

Jacobi could only stand that gaze for so long. His own eyes crept down to note the gun still in Nick's hand. Small beads of sweat were beginning to accumulate on his upper lip. Try as he might, his tongue could not reach them.

Nick let the full effect of it settle before striding purposefully over to the table and leaning in over the German. There were two very definitive sounds that accompanied the action. One, Nick's fist slamming onto the table in front of the man. Two, Wilhelmina slamming down to his right.

The voice, when it came, was arctic. "Let me be blunt. I may be new, but only to you. I've been running missions for more years than I care to recall, and I'm still alive to tell about it. Which is more than I can say for most of the people who have tried to cross me."

A nervous grin flickered across Jacobi's face. Nick ignored it and continued.

"I don't need to hear about schedules, or timetables, or the general dynamics of defections from *anyone*, much less you. I can recite them, chapter and verse. And, as to the state of my emotions, I will relax when I am sitting on the other side of that concrete slab with a Glenfiddich in my hand. Do I make myself clear?"

The nod was adamant, but the smile had faded considerably. The sweat that had begun dotting his lip was being mirrored in tiny beads of moisture spreading over the brow. Nick paused only a second before continuing.

"As for your Dealer, I will reserve judgment until later. Four successes in nine attempts is hardly a record worth bronzing. But I'm not here to give out awards. I'm here to see why three agents have lost their lives working this particular network, *and* I'm here to see that two very valuable scientific minds make it over to the side of the angels. Why your precious Dealer felt it necessary to throw two Polish dissidents into the picture thoroughly baffles me, but I'll live with it if the whole comes in *on time*, and *under budget*. Do I make myself clear?''

Jacobi slumped back into his chair, his body trying for nonchalance, but indicating retreat. ''*Ja, ja,* whatever you wish. You are Mercury. I am told to obey, and I obey.''

''Precisely,'' Nick muttered. ''And now, if you'll excuse me, I'm going to take a short trip up to the roof. Wait here.''

''But—but—'' Jacobi stammered, but he was cut off by the slamming of the door behind Nick.

In the hall, Nick took a deep breath. His original orders had been to wait in the room until delivery. But the script had been torn up right along with the timetable. Delays might have their explanations. After all, defection was not a gentleman's sport. But if the years had taught Nick nothing else, one lesson had been learned. Trust instinct. And, right now, those instincts were screaming that the whole show was up for grabs.

Nick made his way quickly up one flight of stairs and let himself out onto the roof. With only the slightest stooping of his body, he raced to the nearest ledge and began a cautious circling of the area.

First came the back. Nick peered over, scanning the narrow ribbon of alley five floors below. Then he studied the houses that shared the throughway, eyeing each window for any sign of unusual activity. So far, so good.

He then gave quick reconnaissance to the two flanking rooftops. Both were set slightly lower than the building he occupied, and neither offered anything to speak of in the way of cover. If danger lurked at all, it was still buried beneath the slate-topped roofs.

Finally he returned to the front of the building, studying, once more, the barren landscape of the wall. A patrol car cruised by, very deliberate, very slow. Its headlights cast odd patterns of light through the wooden fence to its left and sent odd sparkles of light shimmering across the wire fence to its right. But that was the extent of it. With plodding deliberateness, it continued on its way with hardly a hint of suspicion.

For the briefest second, Nick let his arms rest on the parapet, his mind arguing with his gut that maybe he was witch-hunting. But just as quickly came a duet of sounds that solidified the whole picture.

First came the loud report of backfire and then the rumbling approach of the flatbed truck. There was a part of Nick's mind that still made computerlike calculations. The faint cackling sound of fowl, the harsh grinding of gears being strained, all those things that said the merchandise was on its way—and in one hell of a hurry.

But it was the second sound that brought him to full alert. The faint grinding of gravel beneath the tread of feet—unexpected company, directly behind him.

Nick spun and dropped to his haunches, his back sliding down the stonework of the overlook, Wilhelmina flying out in front of him to take aim. His finger had pressed the trigger back to that magic millimeter of depth that separated inert ironwork from exploding death.

All that greeted him in return was the taut face and wide eyes of Jacobi. "*Nein*!" the man cried. "It is me! Please, they are coming. We should go, *ja*?"

For a second Nick held his aim, the hard breathing of the rotund German treading the air. Nick watched as Jacobi gestured feebly back toward the staircase opening.

The fat German was plodding and obsequious to a fault. But he was far from harmless.

In that one fleeting second when Nick had first turned, he had read something in Jacobi's eyes—something that raised the hackles on the back of Nick's neck. He had read betrayal. The German's hands had not quite made the commitment, but the beady little eyes had, and Nick had caught it.

The question now was whether or not the German knew he had been read. Nick gambled that he did not.

Nick slid Wilhelmina back into her sheath under his arm and stood. "Don't ever surprise me again," he spat. "Next time, I may make a mistake."

Jacobi nodded, the first hint of earnest reaction he had yet displayed.

"Downstairs," clipped Nick. "We've got work to attend to."

Jacobi turned and waddled through the opening. Nick followed. They made it down to the first landing, the landing that housed the room they had so recently been occupying, when Nick halted.

"The cup," he said. "Did you clear it?" Jacobi stared at him, his brows furrowing in apparent confusion. "Check the room," Nick barked and started down the steps. "I'll head on down and wait for you."

Jacobi shrugged and moved toward the room. Nick took the next half-landing at a measured pace, not slow enough to arouse suspicions, but fast enough to get out of sightlines. Nick counted, tallying the seconds with no more than his uncanny ability to assess the German's skills.

Then—instant replay!

Nick turned again, his back once more sliding—this time down plaster—his gun once more filling his hand—this time with different results.

Jacobi turned the corner the very second Nick spun. Unlike the roof, there was no lack of understanding. Jacobi knew what he was dealing with. Fortunately, so did Nick. The German's arm swung around the corner, his machine pistol zeroing in on Nick's skull—at least where it should have been.

The burst chewed at the walls of the stairwell, plaster

cascading down over Nick's head. But plaster was all that touched him. Wilhelmina answered the challenge, beating out three crisp notes that left their mark on the German's chest.

Jacobi's face turned sullen, then confused, as his mind tried to understand the agony that no amount of fat could cushion. His arm slumped to his side, the gun clattering to the floor. His eyes flickered to Nick's, registering honest disbelief, and then two hundred and forty pounds of flesh toppled down the stairs, careening off the banisters with an almost eerie grace.

Nick cursed under his breath. He now knew how three agents had lost their lives. He also knew that if the Dealer's man, Jacobi, was a phony, so was the Dealer.

Before the body had even touched bottom, Nick was up and moving. He raced down the remaining flights, propelled along by two certainties. First, the whole show was a setup. The Dealer had either turned the entire group over to the KGB or he *was* the KGB. The network was penetrated, the formula transparent. Let enough lightweights through to maintain credibility, but make sure you're in place to close the gates on the solid gold.

Second, there were two very golden scientists on a flatbed truck, and, by God, Nick was determined to get them out alive, or go down trying.

There was little time to work out any kind of counterstrategy. Nick was playing their table, in their casino, and the Dealer knew where all the aces were. There was really only one choice. Outside was a truck, and no matter where the enemy had set himself up, it was a hell of a lot harder to hit a moving target than a stationary one.

Nick took the final landing and hit the apartment vestibule in full stride. No sooner had his feet touched the floor than the door at the end of the corridor opened, the truck's driver peeking in to check out the situation.

Was the driver part of the double-cross, or was he one of the clay pigeons?

A suddenly widened pair of eyes and a rapidly darting hand were judge and jury all wrapped up in one. Wilhelmina barked once more. The man's face caved in beneath the impact of the 9mm slug.

Nick slowed himself only long enough to scoop up the victim's machine pistol and several clips. Then he headed, hell-bent, for the door.

He stood deep in the shadows of a recessed doorway. The cowllike collar of his greatcoat was high, and it wrapped around his head, completely obscuring his profile. A wide-brimmed hat further hid his face in shadow. Now and then, when he moved, a shaft of illumination from a nearby streetlight lit up two intense blue eyes. The rest of the face was a montage of shadow and gray-flecked beard.

On extremely close inspection, one could see that the beard was false. But few, if any, had ever gotten close enough to inspect the beard, or the face beneath it.

The Dealer took a long drag on his cigarette, a Russian brand, as harsh and demanding as the country that made it. He was not even conscious of his having cupped the tip, containing the orange glow within the confines of his hand.

His mind was on this new one they had sent, this one code-named *Mercury*.

Not like the others, this one. All those eager American agents, so intent on saving humanity, so eager to accept the Dealer's every arrangement, every detail, as though their morality were a shield of invulnerability.

So many dead angels.

But not this Mercury. He dares to dictate, to demand. And he bargains shrewdly, this one. A safe house with exposed perimeters, a mere block and a half from the breakthrough point. The breakthrough point itself, a sudden tangle of old apartments that interrupted the chain of fences and mine fields to reach out and caress the concrete wall itself—boarded up and guarded, to be sure, but far less exposed, with only human enemies to defeat.

But no matter. Traps can be set anywhere.

Yes, Mercury is not like the others. He is cold, calculating—a machine. He has to die, of course, and there was no time to set up an *accident*. His death will blow the operation; but then, after this night, this defection, the operation will no longer be needed.

He dropped the cigarette and ground it out beneath his heel. Like Mercury, he thought, extinguished.

His glance lifted to the idling truck where it had come to rest three houses away.

The chickens had come to roost. Three of them, at least. One of them would make it over. He had work to do. It would be a dramatic escape, but Jacek would make it to freedom. Free to bury himself deep within the body of the Western enemy, like the mole he was to become.

He watched with interest as the driver of the truck stepped down from his perch and entered the building. Behind him came the faint crackling of a walkie-talkie, and then the voice of his assistant, Yuri. It was an irritating, nasal voice; the Moscow winters seemed to live perpetually in Yuri's sinuses. His identification completed, Yuri sniffed and then passed on the information.

"The driver is entering the building."

The Dealer's answer contained no sarcasm, merely bored detachment. "I have eyes, Yuri. I can see."

"Yes, sir."

There was a moment of silence as the Dealer savored his setup. The agent on the rider's side of the cab opened his door and leaned out onto the running board. He pulled out a penlight and pointed it one apartment house farther up the street. The Dealer watched the tip glow faintly—like a cigarette—three times.

All were aboard.

From behind the Dealer came another crackle of electronics, another muted conversation, and another loud sniffle. The Dealer saved his minion the effort.

"I know, Yuri, I know."

Then came the shot, the sharp crack of gunfire that tagged the Dealer's heart like a whip. From out of the door flew a black-jacketed object, a machine pistol in its left hand, a pistol in its right. With blurring speed, the object leaped onto the running board of the driver's side. There were two more cracks, and the agent with the penlight dropped to the pavement.

The black jacket disappeared into the cab of the truck, not stopping to close the doors. The grinding of gears echoed off the stone facades. With one giant lurch, the truck slipped into gear and jolted off down the street.

With far less fanfare, the Dealer too slipped into motion.

"The car, Yuri!" he barked. "Tell the others. Mercury has flown! Seal off the sector, but maintain Condition Yellow. Repeat, Yellow! Provide resistance—we must make it look good at all costs."

"Mercury is alive," came the voice through the crackling static.

"I know that, you fool. We'll switch to the alternate plan."

"And Mercury?"

"We'll have to let him live, now," the Dealer rasped. "He will now be our means of verification on the other side."

The Dealer clicked off the instrument, and his lips creased in a smile. He had guessed right; Jacobi had been no match for this Mercury.

Often, he thought, it is wise not to reveal all one's plans, even to those carrying them out.

As he stepped into the street, he made a mental note to send a memo of commendation to Jacobi's widow through regular KGB channels.

Nick took the bend in the road, coaxing the ancient vehicle into second gear, his mind clicking off the possibilities. There was no point in going on as scheduled. If the safe house was infested, the breakthrough had to be overrun. The best hope seemed to be to keep on moving and wait for an opening to develop.

He located the first street on his left, slammed the truck into third, and took the corner. The door on his side slammed shut from the sheer momentum. The door on the other side flew open, creaking on its hinges. It then made abrupt contact with the nearest lamp post, successfully tearing it from the truck's body. With it went about twenty chicken coops, wood and feathers flying to litter the cobbles behind.

The street before him was narrow but straight. Nick slipped the truck into fourth and gunned the engine, turning into the heart of the Eastern sector, hoping to put distance between himself and whoever might be behind. At the same time he reached down to the seat on his right, picked up the machine pistol by its barrel, and slammed the stock into the cab's rear window. He was going to need help up front, and there was only one source for that.

Half turning, he screamed through the fractured glass. "Anyone back there speak English?"

A face lifted cautiously into his rearview mirror. It did not belong to either of the scientists, and it was a bit too old to be the boy artist.

"Jacek, right?" Nick yelled. "You speak English?"

It took a moment or two for the terror in the eyes to abate, but the answer was firm. "Yes. Very well, in fact. I was a professor of English at the University of Cracow."

"Lovely," answered Nick. "Can you use one of these?" He held up the machine pistol.

The look of terror returned for an instant, then the man nodded. "I can certainly try. What do I do with it?"

Nick thrust it back through the opening in the glass, his voice bellowing to be heard above the din of the engine. "Use the butt to break out the rest of the window, then climb up here. Tell whoever's nearest you to drag the others as close to this cab as possible and then join you up here. We'll need someone to load clips. Now move!"

Nick threw up the collar on his jacket and eyed the rearview mirror with approval as the dissident followed the orders.

The stock slammed into the remaining glass, sending reflective meteors sailing into the cab. The head then vanished for a moment. When it reappeared, it was climbing its way into the cab. What the climb lacked in grace, it more than made up for in speed.

Nick nodded. "Okay, professor, class time. Wedge yourself in good. It's going to be a bumpy ride. Put your feet there, and there," he pointed. His finger than jabbed at the gun. "The safety's off. Just jam it into your shoulder and pull the trigger. Aim low. The gun will rise on you when firing. And don't clamp the trigger. Run it in short bursts. We'll need to conserve ammo."

"How do I aim?" asked the man.

"Don't worry about it," Nick shouted. "All I need from you is cover. If you see anything that even remotely looks hostile, spray it. If they're busy ducking, they can't get a good shot at us. If you hit 'em, that's gravy."

At that moment, another face loomed into the mirror, a boyish, tow-headed youth who immediately joined them in the cab, a far more graceful entry than the first man's. The boy settled in, and Nick tossed Wilhelmina into the youth's lap, along with several clips—three for the machine pistol, five for the Luger.

"Does painter boy here have any idea how to load these?" Nick called over to Jacek.

To Nick's delight and relief, the boy replied for himself, in English. "I have never done this, but learning must be easy, yes?"

Nick allowed a quick smile. "Hang onto the optimism, kid. We'll need it." He then gave a crash course in weaponry, watching with approval as the boy snapped in the hardware with a flourish. There was only time for the quickest of "hot damns" before the enemy made his appearance.

Two streets up ahead, a military Jeep sped by, hit its

brakes, and then jerked back to block the road. The Jeep's three occupants leaped out, guns sliding off their shoulders into eager hands. Nick immediately downshifted, noting the next turnoff, and yelled to the young artist. "Everyone packed up against the cab back there?"

The boy nodded.

Nick turned back and shouted, "Hang on, folks. Things are liable to get a bit hairy." He then turned back, steeling himself as the three soldiers down the street began shouldering arms. "Okay, professor, it's all yours."

With that, he rammed the wheel to the left, the front wheel brushing the curb, the truck screaming as it tilted into the turn. Another dozen cages broke from their moorings to scatter around them. At the same time, the professor went into high gear. Nick watched as the man fired, sending the three soldiers diving for cover. He then drove the shift back into fourth and left the first obstacle behind.

"Good job, professor," Nick grinned. "Didn't hit any soldiers, but I counted at least three chickens pulverized. We'll notch the stock at the first opportunity."

Both Jacek and the boy smiled in relieved appreciation. But none of the smiles were to be long-lived. In front of Nick appeared another vehicle screeching to block the road. This one was civilian, a black Simca, barely large enough to fill the crossroads before them. From out of the car scrambled two figures, gray-coated and smelling of State Security. Nick gauged the odds and made his commitment.

As the two men reached into their coats for pistols, Nick jammed the gears, giving the appearance of stopping. Just as quickly, he lifted the clutch and floored the pedal. There was a burst of backfire, and then the roar of the engine as the truck bore down on the two security men like an elephant gone haywire. The men fired several rounds in panic, but none of the shots found its mark. Instead there was only the agonizing screech of metal as the truck plowed through the rear end of the tiny car. Nick gripped the wheel to retain control and then sped on.

Far up ahead loomed another obstacle. There was a faint glow of a street lamp and the linear pattern of light spilling through slatted boards. Nick recognized it immediately. It was the first stage in the grotesque barrier known as the Berlin Wall. From his right he felt the cab's other two occupants staring at him.

Nick deliberated for only an instant. The streets were a crap shoot. Sooner or later there would be something in front of them that could neither be moved nor avoided. The open road seemed the best bet.

Nick floored the truck again, gaining all the momentum he could. To his right, the breathing became labored and frantic as the wall grew taller and taller in front of them. It was obvious to all that Nick had no intention of turning.

At the moment of impact, there was only a prolonged whimper from the young painter to punctuate the event.

The truck collided with the fence, bursting through the slats and wire ribbing. There was a slight lift to the front end, and then a terrible groan as one of the twisted supports dug at the vehicle's underbelly. Nick jammed the gears down and twisted the wheel to his right, maintaining equilibrium as the truck careened off the curb and staggered onto the patrol road. Then he gunned it and prayed that there were no vital organs punctured.

His eyes immediately began searching for some way out. The terrain was exactly what he had observed before—tank traps and mine fields to the left. To his right was only the slatted fence, beyond which now traveled several pairs of headlights—all paralleling his movement. There was a brief feeling of despair and frustration, and then something up ahead caught Nick's attention.

Headlights were coming toward him, but they were not yet visible. What he saw instead was the aura of those headlights fanning out from around a large dark mass. Closer inspection of the mass revealed it to be a massive stone structure—a church planted smack in the middle of no man's land, an ecclesiastical bridge that stretched past tank traps and mines, to touch the Western wall on his right.

"Bingo!" he muttered, just as the headlights cleared the bulk and pointed themselves directly toward the truck's grill. "Hunch down," he yelled to his allies. "We're getting past that son-of-a-bitch and walking out of here!"

"How?" gulped the young artist, his head slowly sinking below the dash.

"Easy," Nick replied. "We just play a little game. It's an American classic. It's called 'chicken.' And we'll find out damn quick who really wants to win."

He slammed the pedal to the floor and set the wheels directly for the approaching headlights. Nick, too, lowered himself in his seat, his eyes barely creasing the dashboard surface as he gauged the oncoming vehicle. It was truck-sized, hard to read in the glare of the approaching lights, but looking every bit like a troop carrier.

From above the glare came a burst of light, and Nick slumped himself down hard in the seat. The glass in front of him burst into the cab as several rounds slammed through it. He waited until there was a lull in the fireworks and then peered back up.

The vehicle was a mere one hundred yards away, its siren screeching in short warning blasts. Nick merely shifted the truck back onto collision course. As he drew nearer, the blasts became more frantic, evolving from sounds of warning to sounds of disbelief as Nick's intentions became obvious.

With some twenty yards left, the siren screamed out in supplication and then lost itself in the screech of tires as the troop carrier slid off to the right, missing contact by mere inches.

Nick let out an audible sigh of relief and then propped himself up behind the wheel. The church could now be clearly seen in the glow of his headlights. It was a reddish stone structure that needed only two layers of fence to be reached. But the fence was directly parallel to their angle of flight. There was no way to gain a head-on angle.

It was no time to worry over luxuries. The church was their only hope, and the church was what Nick was determined to reach.

He swung the truck to the left, wincing as wire fencing gripped at the edge of the flatbed. Then he slammed the wheel to the right, gritting his teeth and gripping the controls with every ounce of strength he possessed.

The right front bumper caught the barrier, the headlight exploding as fence posts pounded at it like drumsticks. The truck tried to veer its way back onto the road, but Nick was adamant, forcing the wheel, driving the truck's nose toward safety.

Then from up ahead came another glare of headlights—headlights to match the ones now pursuing from behind.

"Grab, dammit!" Nick bellowed, coaxing fate to join him. "Break through now, you tin-plated son-of-a-bitch!"

Fate must have been listening because the truck gave a sudden lurch, and then—breakthrough.

The right front tire hit the earth with a neck-jarring jolt, then the left, both on the other side of the barrier. Nick gunned the engine, ignoring the conflict of metal on metal as the rear wheels joined their mates.

The second fence still stood before them, but at a much easier angle. It veered in from the Western side, turning to encircle the bulk of the church—a head-on target that offered no problem. Nick gave his last push on the pedal and leveled the final barrier.

There was no need to kill the engine. It gave a loud burst and, with a fanfare of hissing steam, gave up the ghost.

There was little time for exaltation. The nose of the truck stood some ten yards from the brick facade, and Nick was determined to cross as quickly as possible.

"Out! Now!" he cried, pushing at his two neighbors, forcing them out the gaping hole where the door had been. Silently he thanked the fates that not only got him through the fence, but now provided a smoke screen as the steam, pouring from the engine, curled up from beneath the truck to hang foglike outside the door to his left. He filed out behind the dissidents.

"Make for the building!" he shouted. "Shoot the doors open if you have to, but get 'em open, and get 'em wide!"

Nick then cut to his right, moving toward the back of the truck to retrieve the two scientists.

That's when fate gave out.

Not even the accompaniment of steam and sirens could mute the sound from Nick's ears. Too many nights and days on too many battlefields had taught him the hissing sound of a rocket launcher.

Bellowing to the two men to jump to safety, Nick threw himself back behind the cover of the cab and prepared for the concussion of the upcoming blast.

It roared like thunder, but fell far short of the Armageddon Nick had anticipated. The explosion was firm, but muted. Nick rolled free of the truck, and then saw why. Blasting had not been the goal. What the launcher had sent was burning death—a napalm-filled incendiary that was gnawing away at the bed of the truck.

Nick felt his guts sink. Though the blast had not been particularly powerful, it had been more than potent. To the left, twisted on the ground, were the bodies of the two scientists, fire licking up from their remains.

Nick stared at the burning bodies of the two men, and hatred coursed through every bone in his body—hatred for any system that could drive men to run, and stop them with such finality. Hatred for any man who could be a party to such a system. Hatred for the Dealer, the man who set it up.

The Death Dealer.

Cursing under his breath, Nick raised himself and made for the doors of the church. He hit them and flew through just as a barrage of bullets went to work on the stone facing of the entry.

"Aim higher, idiots! We are trying to put on a good show, not decimate the cast!"

The Dealer clicked off the button on the walkie-talkie and thrust it into Yuri's lap. His fingers came back to pinch at the bridge of his nose as he fought to regain control of his emotions.

Dogs, he thought, East German dogs! Tear down the bloody wall and let them all run to the West. It would have to be the most collectively destructive act ever perpetrated by the Eastern Alliance.

With a sigh, his fingers dropped and his eyes returned to the church entry. "He is in?" he murmured.

"*Da,*" came the sniffled response.

"Then let us move in and complete the charade. Order the idiots to file through the breech. But no one, and I mean *no one*, is to fire unless I order it. Make that very clear, Yuri."

The Dealer pushed open the door and moved from the car. Behind came his associate, mimicking the orders into the two-way radio. The Dealer moved quickly, racing through the torn fencing and stopping only to stare at the twin fires that used to be men.

To the degree that they were dead, the mission had not been a disaster. The Dealer could even find room for some self-admiration. The fire launchers that had killed them were his own invention, one of the myriad ideas that had helped him rise on the competitive ladder of the KGB infrastructure. Lessen the explosive charges, he had told them. Not enough impact to breach the walls, but more than enough to blow up fragile human bodies. And fire, comrades; let them feel the terror of *fire*.

The rumbling of nearby troops brought him back from his reverie. He turned and gestured, guiding half the men around the far side of the building and the other half down the near side. He let the second group sprint past him. All of them moved like specters through the thick fog, with the Dealer close behind.

The soldiers cleared the side of the building and came up short. Rifles flew to their shoulders, crosshairs trained on something center and relatively high up. The Dealer turned the corner and saw what it was. High atop the last twelve-foot barrier, his arms stretched back to help the young artist, was Mercury himself.

With the sound of rifle bolts being thrown into readiness, the action on the wall came to a freeze.

"Halt!" came the Dealer's voice. "Do not fire!"

The Dealer gave a quick scan of the area below the wall. No Jacek! That could only mean that he was already over the wall. The Dealer could almost hear the young artist demanding that his loving friend be the first to climb. Such were the uses of friendship.

"Hit the floods!" the Dealer cried, his voice noticeably lower now, almost a growling rasp.

In an instant, the area around the figures on the wall was turned from night into day by powerful lights. The young artist dangled, his wrists in Mercury's grasp.

The Dealer's grip tightened on the butt of the Walther. Now, he thought, to play out the last act.

Jacek had demanded the boy's safety. It was part of the price for years of future dedication. It was a price that had to be met. As for Mercury, he, too, was needed on the other side. Needed to get Jacek to America, to tell of the narrow escape, to plant the mole where he would blossom and grow in the years ahead.

The Dealer pushed his way between two of the soldiers and marched up to the wall. Mercury responded with devious subtlety. His right hand slipped from the boy's wrist; in it, a pistol. The muzzle came to rest on what he could see of the Dealer's forehead. The Dealer merely ignored it, tucking his own pistol into his coat as he came to a halt in the shadow beneath the dangling man.

The Dealer did nothing more dramatic than grab the

young man's leg, his eyes coming up to meet the burning gaze of the enemy agent. "The fourth one is on the other side, yes?"

Mercury held the other man's gaze and nodded.

"Then you have a portion of the victory tonight," said the Dealer. "That, and your life. Take both and go." Mercury did not move. "The boy will not be shot. You have my word on it. He will be spared."

"On whose authority," came the clipped reply.

"You have the word of the Dealer."

Mercury's head moved slowly from side to side. "No. Not the Dealer. The Death Dealer!"

A faint sparkle of surprise gleamed in the Russian's eyes. The Death Dealer! It had a ring to it, a sound that brought a certain joy to the man at the base of the wall. "Yes," he muttered. "I suppose so. To some. But not to this one. That I can promise you."

Nick narrowed his eyes into slits. No matter how he concentrated his stare, he couldn't evade the glare of the searchlights. And even if he could, he doubted that he would be able to see much more of the Dealer's face than a flash of beard and the glowing coals of his eyes.

Nick debated a moment longer and then released his grip on the young man's wrist. The boy slid to the ground, the Dealer's arm snaking across his shoulder in a gesture that was faintly paternal. His charge firmly in hand, the Dealer's eyes returned to Nick.

"Till the next time, my friend," he said.

"Till the next time," echoed Nick, backing himself off the wall and dropping down to safety.

The dream was quite vivid. The young artist was hanging, cold hands holding him from above, cold eyes grabbing at him from below. There were rumbling sounds, like talking, but none of it intelligible. All the dreamer knew was that the sounds held his fate in the balance.

And then the rumbling stopped and the hands were

gone, and he was falling—miles and miles of falling. He waited for the cold eyes to catch him, but they never did. He looked down, ready to greet his tormentor, but the eyes were gone.

Instead, there was only infinite nothingness.

Stefan screamed out in his sleep, doing his utmost to rouse himself in the bed. He blinked his eyes in a habitual effort to clear them, but there was nothing to clear them for. Around him was nothing but inky blackness, as though the dream had risen with him.

He lifted his hand and stuck it in front of his eyes. Nothing. At best, a faint image of fingers moving, an image that could owe as much to imagination as it could to any fragments of reflected light.

Then Stefan sighed.

Sensory deprivation, he thought. The first thing they tell you of. If you are caught, they warned, they will interrogate. They will try to find out names and places. But first, they will break you down, destroy your will to resist. You will spend hours, days, in the black box. There will be no sounds, nothing to see, nothing to touch or smell. Just the interminable blackness that will tear at your soul.

Stefan let his hand drop. He was ready for it—ready for *them*. He would fight them all, spurred on by the knowledge that Jacek, at least, had made it. "Have a beer for me," he whispered into the darkness. "And a woman too, my friend."

"No doubt he is doing that right now."

The voice startled Stefan. His head spun in the direction from which it had come, his hands tightening on the bedclothes beneath him. It was a familiar voice, the voice of betrayal. Somewhere in the blackness, maybe only a few feet away, was the Dealer.

Stefan moved with deliberateness. It was pitch black in the room, but it was the same for both men. There was a score to settle. Stefan leaped toward the spot from which the voice had come, his hands outstretched to grip the throat of the man who peddled death.

His only reward was a stabbing pain in the belly as his enemy sunk a fist deep into his midsection. Stefan staggered, but refused to crumple. He stood a moment, fighting for breath, listening for the slightest rustle that would tell him where the Dealer had moved. He heard a voice instead.

"You are angry. You should not be. You are alive when you could be dead. That should carry some gratitude, I would think."

Stefan moved again, rushing at the voice, determined to reach his tormentor. But again his only reward was pain, another crippling blow to the belly that no amount of determination could shake off. And then a second blow, the sharp contact of a cupped hand slapped against his ear.

Stefan went down, bowing to his knees, his brain screaming from the pain inside his head. There were a few seconds as the ringing in his ears settled, seconds in which he wondered at the man's ability to function in the dark. But questions subsided with the pain. What was left was hatred.

"Turn on the lights," Stefan hissed. "Meet me as an equal. I will kill you, I swear it. Kill you with my bare hands."

There was only a mirthless chuckle for response. "But there *are* lights. Light is everywhere. Surely you know that."

Behind the words came a sound, the familiar rustle of curtains opening. Stefan rose and followed the sound, stopping only when his hands collided with glass. He moved them around, feeling the smooth surface, testing it, absorbing with growing horror the sensation of heat radiating off the panes.

And the heat followed him, pursuing him relentlessly as

he fell to his knees, tears brimming in his eyes.

The only coldness in that room was the voice of the Dealer.

"You see, my boy—sunlight. Rich, golden sunlight." There was a moment's pause as the voice grew quieter. "But then you can't see, can you. No, you can't. Nor will you ever—ever again."

CHAPTER ONE

SPRING 1983

THE AUSTRIAN-CZECHOSLOVAK FRONTIER

Ghosts! Nick mused. All around me, ghosts.

He gave a slight shiver and ran the hood up on his assault parka. It was less a concession to the eerie twists of thought than it was to the very earthly spring winds that gusted down the mountain, breezes that carried strong remembrances of their origin in the snow-capped peaks behind.

The landscape possessed its own ghostly ambience; there was no denying that. Behind Nick were the Sumava Mountains, mottled in shadow and moonlight. Around him, the thick, dark carpet of spruce and larch that constituted the Bohemian Forest. Below, the Vltava River, arching its way toward the distant capital of Prague, its waters churning beneath the volume of spring thaw, the first faint tendrils of fog drifting out to engulf the landscape.

It was an environment that invited fantasy. Bohemia had authored more than its share of childhood terrors. It was a land peopled by werewolves and vampires and castles that echoed with the sound of human screaming.

But that was the stuff of cinema.

Nick Carter could ignore those flights of imagination. He was, after all, an agent—a Killmaster. And there were rituals that accompanied any mission, rituals designed to prepare, and divert: the occasional surveillance of the terrain, guaranteeing one's aloneness; the methodical checks on the Skorpion 61 submachine gun; the retracing in one's mind of the escape route back to the safety of Austria. All these, designed to keep the mission in clear focus.

But ghosts are persistent entities, especially when divorced from landscape and shadow. The ghosts that haunted Nick were his own, born of memory and history. He glanced at his watch, noting the lateness. Then he returned his eyes to the trail and clearing below. In his mind, the spectral haunting of history, the curse of a photographic memory.

You are restive, Herr Mercury. We have been running our little railroad for many years now—trust us. You cannot run on schedules, ja? You will learn . . . you will learn . . . you will learn.

Words from a dead man. Words from a defection that ended in bitter disappointment—a defection not unlike the one that Nick was now awaiting. There were differences, to be sure. Differences of venue, of intent, of accumulated experience. But there were similarities, too, one very big one in particular. And it was this that teased at the corners of Nick's imagination.

As defections go, this one was a motley array. Seven Poles were making their bid for freedom, running from the iron hand of martial law. Four were complete unknowns, and two possessed only moderate acclaim: poets whose concepts were not nearly as irritating to the Russians as was their verse. All in all, a routine transit operation that even the clowns at Central Intelligence could manage. Hardly a job for AXE.

No, it was the one remaining who had cried out for Nick's attendance, a ghostly voice pleading for Mercury to attend him. It was a cry that implicated other apparitions. It hinted of information, of possibilities, of elimination.

It spoke of the Death Dealer.

And Nick responded, dusting off the ancient alias of Mercury, and wending his way into the Bohemian heartland. And he was waiting, praying that one living ghost could indeed point a bony finger at the other. There was a debt to settle, a thirteen-year-old promise to be fulfilled. The Death Dealer was already dead; he just needed Nick Carter to escort him to the grave.

From off in the distance came a fitting counterpoint to Nick's reveries. It was the cry, made hollow by the vast expanse of valley, of a night hawk. Nick sat up, staring at a moon growing ever more hazy, hoping to glimpse the bird's distant silhouette. He spotted it, circling in the air, its predatory wings outstretched—a death dealer by nature.

Then he looked back down the trail, searching the distance for the faintest hint of headlights. There would be no flatbed truck this time, no squabbling of chickens. Just a minibus filled with frightened men. And there would be no disappointments. Spotting no lights, Nick shifted his gaze to the terrain, assuring himself once more of his solitude. It was a rendezvous well chosen, devoid of humanity and government scrutiny.

Content, Nick settled back into his niche, his tiny corner of the shadowed forest, and let his thoughts wander for a brief moment. He tried to imagine what his ghostly summoner must look like today. Memory offered an image blurred somewhat by the circumstances of their previous meeting. There was the boyish smile laden with optimism and the shock of sandy hair. There were the delicate fingers, painter's fingers, jamming home clips with a flourish, and hands that clung deftly and tenaciously to his own. There was youth, there was bravado, and finally, there was resignation.

Those were the things that Nick recalled the most about Stefan Borczak. But he had spent too many years in the field to fool himself into thinking that those were the features he would shortly confront. What had been a boy in his twenties, only thirteen years ago, would now be a man far older in appearance. They all were, these runaways from oppression. The Dealer had promised a life, not a lifetime. The Soviet system could take the gift of life and make it a sentence far crueler than its alternative.

No, Nick thought, the man I greet shortly will be a far cry from the boy I dropped at the wall. A ghost, no more.

That night came back to him, and with it, another image. The Dealer, the man he had rechristened in the gloom of the red-bricked church. And, photographic memory or not, it was an image that refused to crystallize with any clarity. Other details were far clearer: the wail of sirens, the clatter of rifles readied and pointed in his direction, the flickering glow of firelight playing up and down the Dealer's side; those images were very clear.

But the face had eluded him, burying itself in the shadow of the hat, the shadow of the church, the shadow of the wall. All, that is, but the eyes. Those had somehow found their own light, radiating from the depths of shadow to print themselves forever in Nick's memory. It was the hateful light of those eyes, cold and possessive, that Nick was committed to seeing extinguished.

And it was not a commitment built on one night alone. In thirteen years, there had been other encounters. The night at the wall had been a minor victory for Nick. The scientists had been lost, but the network had been exposed. The Dealer found himself out of the freedom market.

But the Dealer was a climber of the first order. He had apparently taken Nick's christening to heart, making the switch from agent to assassin with ease. The Death Dealer became more than just an accusation, it became a reality, a meteoric career built on the bones of any who incurred the wrath, or envy, of the Soviet system. It was a ghostly reality that had returned to haunt Nick more than once.

Six times, to be exact. Four had resulted in victories for the Dealer, two in victories for Nick. And the last time? A draw, for lack of a better word: two lives retained, but at the cost of very sensitive information. Four disappointments, two celebrations, and one near confrontation that almost brought the man within Nick's sights.

"Next time," Nick muttered, "there will be no 'almost.' I'll have you. I'll put out those lights forever."

Loud squawking from the night hawk population drew his attention skyward. He craned his neck, again seeking out the moon, again seeking silhouettes in the thickening fog. This time the hawks were much closer, and many more strong in numbers. In spite of the hazy overgrowth, Nick saw what he needed. There were five birds circling in a wild dance.

But at no point in the parade of shadows that passed through the lunar spotlight was there even the dimmest hint of quarry. No rabbits gripped in the viselike press of talons, no squirrels lifting off the forest floor in feathered balloons. Just movement, and confusion, and the clarion cry of warning.

Nick was no longer alone.

He jerked up in place, his eyes flying back down the landscape below. In the distance he could make out the faintest glow of headlights. It was scarcely a glimmer, an aura transmitted through the reflective curtain of fog, far too distant to stir the local avian population into such disturbance.

No, it was the foreground that held the answer, and Nick searched with eyes as deadly as any hawk's. It took a second or two, but slowly a picture began to emerge, a picture which caused grave concern. Dimly at first, and then with nearing accuracy, Nick could see a small column of Czech soldiers picking its way through the night. They cleared the forest's edge, about two dozen of them, and then hustled their way to the clearing below. It was here that they halted, one man stepping away to note the distant glow of headlights.

Nick needed no further encouragement. Another ghost had risen to join him. He threw himself onto his belly and snaked his way down the mountainside, aiming at a thick stand of granite, one of the several outcroppings of rock that scarred the terrain. He chewed on the reality of what was occurring below, and it left a bitter taste in his mouth. Another network too porous and leaky to survive; another defection threatened by betrayal.

The image of the boy he had deserted so many years before at the Berlin Wall filled his brain. There would be no repeats, no reruns. Too many possibilities were riding in that minibus.

He reached the stone face, laying his Skorpion at the bottom, and carefully eased himself up the rocky spine. Slowly he peered over the summit, availing himself of the improved perspective.

Below, the column leader was distributing his charges, blanketing the area at the trail's end. Ten of the soldiers took their orders and then raced off to another stone facade on the left. Another ten shot off to the right, crossing the trail and setting up crossfire positions from a stand of spruce trees. The leader and one remaining man waited until everyone was planted before turning and striding up the hillside.

Another ghost had risen. The approaching soldier labored up the incline, a portable rocket launcher seesawing over his shoulder. In his other hand, a box of rockets. It was obvious that prisoners were not part of the game plan. The two continued on, finally halting behind the cover of an outsized boulder. Once in place, preparations moved swiftly. The launcher came to rest on its stony base, the box of rockets opened for the coming slaughter.

A quick glance down the road gave Nick his time frame. What had been a distant aura of headlights was now an approaching glow. There were maybe three minutes left before the vehicle would screech to a halt, smack in the middle of ground zero. It was not a lot of time, but it was all Nick had.

He gave the terrain a quick reading. Nature was on his side. The group to the left had the better cover, but by far the less secure position. Behind them, the mountain face took a sharp rise, culminating in a broad shelf of exposed granite that gave every appearance of being in the final stages of defeat against the winter frosts and weathering. A note of hope sounded in Nick's not-too-optimistic chest.

He knew, from the moment he saw it, that the rocket launcher would be his first goal. This was not the Berlin Wall; mountains held no fear of breaching. The charges in the box would be full—and deadly. But mountains could be altered. With enough coaxing, the rock face might be persuaded to release its grip. If that were so, the men stationed beneath stood little chance of surviving the results.

Nick then turned to his right, studying the possibilities at the forest's edge. The men there were in a slightly better position. Although more exposed from Nick's angle, they were much more scattered, and harder to eliminate as a body. The best bet was still the rocket launcher. If he could pound a few of the tree bases, concentrating his fire in the center of their position, he might be lucky enough to claim a few of the enemy in the resultant collapse of timber.

If not, it would still serve as a diversion, and a potent threat to men expecting little resistance. If any of them were prone to panic, they might just flush themselves out into the open. From there, the Skorpion would do the work. It wasn't foolproof, but it would have to do on short notice.

Nick swiveled and slid down the stone perch, his feet touching silently on the ground. He lifted the Skorpion, throwing it over his head and cinching the strap tight against his body. He took a few precious seconds to regulate his breathing—deep, calming breaths of air that quieted his nerves and sharpened his concentration. The time for determinations was over. The commitment was made. That left only the doing. The machine had taken over. Nick slipped from the shadow of the rock and started his trek down the hill.

Time forced him to move more quickly and more openly than desired, but the fog proved to be a salvation—the fog and the almost hypnotic concentration of the Czech soldiers on the approaching lights. Nick zigzagged his way from tree to tree, angling toward the two men below, his feet gliding quietly across the soft carpet of grass.

As he went, he gave the required twists of the wrist necessary to release Hugo from his chamois perch against his forearm. The pencil-thin stiletto slipped silently into his hand, its blade cupped gently in the palm to keep even the faintest hint of light from glinting out a warning.

Nick came to a halt about ten meters from the waiting leader and his deadly playmate. The trip, from this point on, would have to be far more cautious if suspicions were not to be aroused. The remaining distance offered no cover. Nick once more slipped to his belly, slithering his way forward with infinite patience.

He was aided in his efforts by the continuous drone of the leader's voice as he commented on the vehicle's approach on a walkie-talkie. The man stood peering over the fronting boulder while his crony remained hunched behind, his fingers toying nervously with the rocket launcher.

Nick crawled to within a foot of the stooped figure and waited for the next outburst of communication. It came within seconds. Nick moved. His hand clamped across the kneeling man's mouth while Hugo explored the terrain of his throat. Steel skating on butter. The chatter generated by the leader's mounting excitement was more than ample cover for the thin whistle of air that accompanied the man's death.

Slowly Nick laid the body on the ground, and again he waited; this time for the leader to hit a natural stopping point in his reporting. It would not do to have him cut off in the middle of his discourse.

From below came the chugging sounds of the minibus as the Czech called out his final commands and clicked the radio into silence. Then, with all the panache of martinets everywhere, he thrust the object blindly behind him, waiting for his comrade to dutifully remove it from his hands. Nick obliged him, tossing it off to one side.

His eyes still intent on the scene below, the hand remained outstretched, fingers wiggling impatiently. It was obvious to Nick that the leader wanted the privilege of demolishing the dissidents himself—a gold star for his record, a good deed to increase his standing with his Soviet superiors. It was a hopeful sign. It meant the shooting would not commence below until the leader had had his stab at glory.

This, Nick could not oblige. Hugo darted like a needle, entering the man's hand from the back, lifting out through the palm, and then sliding back through again. The leader's shoulder gave a wincing leap, and his hand flew away to hover before disbelieving eyes. When the head turned, astonishment and hate were waging pitched battle for control of the man's facial muscles. Both were equally defeated when the soldier realized his dilemma. It was not some wicked conscript who faced him now; it was Nick Carter—Nick and Hugo. And although he would never comprehend the who or why of it all, he could recognize death when he faced it.

And death came swiftly. With no more than a sideways flick of the wrist, Nick sent Hugo darting through the air. The stiletto whistled faintly before burying itself in the man's right eye. There was a gasp and an instant of jerking chaos as the blade lodged itself in the man's brain. But this passed quickly. What remained was a useless collection of flesh that toppled forward, its face slamming the ground with a savage finality.

Nick quickly rolled the man over and retrieved Hugo from its human sheath. He neatly cleaned the blade and tucked it back into its nest. Then he stood, replacing the commander at his post, and took in the scene below.

The minibus was coasting to a halt at the trail's end, its headlights blinking out the preordained coding of arrival. In his mind's ear, Nick could hear the responding click of gun chambers from the flanking troops.

Now was the time to test out strategies. Nick reached down and hoisted the box of rockets, parking it on the ledge to his left. He then grabbed the launcher, laying it over the stone like some fossilized tripod. He grabbed one of the rockets and slipped it in the back, his eye coming quickly down to the sight. He was greeted by the sepia shading of infrared technology. He allowed himself the barest twist of a grateful smile as he settled the crossed hairs on the clinging patch of granite to his left.

He fired.

There was a muted pop and the familiar hiss as the launcher bucked against his shoulder. The rocket streaked away, leaving behind its own thick fog of cordite. It trailed off into the distance, a streamer of light behind, as it sought out its target.

Then came the fireworks.

The rocket impacted itself against the stone, its exploding roar raping the stillness of the night. Even before it did, Nick was preparing the backup. His hand dove into the box, seeking out another missile, oblivious to the partition that divided the box in two. He popped the rocket into its silo, only marginally conscious of the small nipple of red that marked its tip. There was an instant of re-aiming, this time his concentration on the stone face that shielded the soldiers. It would not do to have any of them go over the top.

Nick fired again. Once more the production of man collided with the product of nature. Again there was an exploding roar, but this time it was accompanied by a blinding flash of orange-white light and a waterfall of fire that splattered across the stone, and then clung with a determination all its own. Nick could hardly believe the turn of luck.

Napalm!

Nick's head jerked over to inspect the box beside him. Twin compartments, twin alternatives of destruction. One side was neatly stacked with explosives. The other, identical, except for tiny markings of red. Without delay, Nick grabbed for one of the regular rockets. He loaded and fired, once more attacking the clinging stonework above the men. From behind him came the frantic crackling of the walkie-talkie—confused voices seeking clarification from their leader.

The only answer that came was the sudden groaning of stone as the granite shelf gave up its struggle and parted from the mountain. There was a further shrieking as the rocks tumbled down, crumbling into smaller fragments, and finally slamming their way into the ridge that hid the Czech militia.

Nick lowered the launcher and unshouldered his Skorpion, ready for any who might avoid the charge of falling rock. The echoing rumble of the landslide more than overwhelmed the cries of fear and dying from behind the cover. Two men managed to scurry up and over the crest, but their efforts only brought them lead instead of granite. Two quick blasts of the Skorpion sent them dropping into the fires that licked at their feet.

By now, the flank on the right had managed to perceive that they were being opposed. There came a gradually committed shower of gunfire in Nick's direction, but not

before he had managed to slide rockets, launcher, and self
down behind the safety of the boulder.

Nick dropped the Skorpion and readied himself for
phase two of his plan. He picked out three of the specially
marked charges and slipped the first one home. He dove to
his right, clearing the boulder, his belly pounding the
earth as he let the first rocket fly from ground level. He
then rolled back, repeating the process to his left.

Each time the returning gunfire spent itself on where he
had been, not where he was. With each retreat came the
hollow explosions of the rocket blasts, the shimmering
halo of firelight, and the guttural moaning of timber as
another tree would fragment and topple.

For the final launch, Nick went back up top, firing his
missile and delighting as the napalm sought out lumber
and flesh like a hoard of glowing birds. He dropped the
launcher and swept up the Skorpion again, slamming
home a fresh clip in the process.

The napalm was a blessing of the highest order. Those
who were not caught by the fire itself were now lit up in
the glowing conflagration, caught in the fog-piercing
view of the stage lights. Nick opened fire, cutting them
down one by one. Any who managed to avoid the hellfires
were soon greeted by the deadly shower of brimstone.

But that was the good news. The bad news was that the
fires were also illuminating a different picture. Panic was
not limited to the soldiers alone. The dissidents too were
feeling the grip of hysteria. Rather than holding to the
cover and safety of the minibus, they were bolting into the
open. Seven stumbling refugees fleeing the rage of the
battlefield.

What was worse, they had determined Nick as their
salvation and were rushing his position on the hillside,
gradually working their way into the line of fire.

Nick did his best to cry out through the sounds of battle,
screaming for them to drop to the ground, but the voice

just would not reach them. He watched with horror as one of their number collapsed.

They were now fully in the line of fire, leaving Nick only one solution. Exposure. Reluctantly the agent yielded to the demands of the moment. Popping in a fresh clip, he clambered to the top of the boulder and stood to full height. He let loose a barrage of bullets that kicked up the pebbles at the fleeing feet.

Having gotten their attention, he again screamed out his directive. "Drop, damn you! Hit the goddamn ground and stay there!"

There was shock, but there was also response. They dropped to a man, leaving both Nick and the soldiers head on head. Nick refused to allow as much as a millisecond to pass before opening up. Dissident heads had barely dropped from sight when he let fire a shower of bullets that took two of the Czechs instantly. The third managed to carve his initials at Nick's feet, but that was the extent of it. Another Skorpion blast left him dancing backwards until he toppled.

Nick dropped to his knee and swept the terrain, but there were no more challenging barrages. Instead, there was only the popping crackle of burning timber. He jumped from the boulder and ran down to his frightened flock.

Slowly, they rose up, heads turning in disbelief at the carnage around them. And then the heads stopped, each in its turn, each noting the one of their number that did not rise. Nick could sense the mingled emotions of regret and relief that shuddered through them. He stopped himself at the fringe of their grief.

"Who did we lose?" he asked.

The answer was delivered sullenly, an anonymous voice from out of the pack. "Olek," was all that was said. It was tribute and last rite all rolled into one.

Nick could sense the communal idea forming in the

group, but it was his duty to nip it. "Sorry," he said, his voice even but firm. "No time for burials. The fireworks will invite examination. We've got ten kilometers to travel, and we'd better travel it fast."

One by one they turned, their expressions at first reproachful. But just as quickly, each registered an understanding. Mercury was their leader and he knew what was best. Nick watched each of the faces, noting them, studying them, searching out the one that matched the photo in his mind.

The first four faces were more or less what Nick had expected—older men, features lined from years of fighting the impossible. The fifth face carried with it some surprise. It was a woman's face, early into her thirties, but almost ravishing in its beauty. It was pale and high cheekboned, framed by raven black hair and punctuated by dark onyx eyes.

Nick found himself riveted to the face, his attention only straying when a voice reached out to grab him. "So, Mercury, we meet once more. This time with happier results."

Nick turned toward the voice and found himself as close to startled as he would ever be. Whatever changes he had imagined for the boy in his mind, he was not prepared for what reality provided him. The hair that had been sandy was now snow white, and the face that had once held such sparkle, now held only thick lines of contempt.

But it was the eyes that Nick had not expected, dead, stony eyes with hints of gray around the whites—the eyes of a blind man. Nick watched with morbid fascination as the eyes peered lamely over his shoulder.

"You are silent, my friend. You are no doubt marveling at the sincerity of the Dealer's promises. Grant a life, but make it a living hell. Take the eyes from the artist, and you own him. Is that not so?"

Nick could not be certain that there was not a hint of recrimination in the voice. He answered it with measured care. "He'll pay, Stefan. I promised myself then, and I promise you now. He'll pay."

There was the barest hint of a smile. His hand came up, in it a cane, its handle an ornately carved fist. The handle came gently to rest on Nick's arm as the man spoke.

"That he will, my friend. That is a promise I make you. Hela!" The blind man called to the woman, waiting until he felt the touch of her arm on his own before continuing. "My wife will guide me. I believe we still have a journey ahead. I will not delay us with details—or infirmities. Lead on, my friend."

"Let's move," Nick echoed, as he turned and marched the group toward Austria, and freedom.

The two men watched the tiny parade blend into the distant trees, safe behind the cover of the forest. Rankov lowered his binoculars and let them come to rest against his bulging belly. Next to him was the Czech officer, his own binoculars still surveying the damage below.

"God in heaven," came the muttered comment.

Rankov chuckled at the unconscious heresy. "Careful, comrade. Religion is the first sign of deteriorating values. I shall have to report you if you persist."

But the jibe was lost in the survey of bodies and fires below. The glasses finally slipped from the man's eyes. "Twenty men—destroyed. By whom? By what?"

Rankov shrugged. "By Mercury, as he was once called. By Nick Carter, if you prefer. No matter what name, the results are identical. Impressive, is it not?"

The Czech only stared, his mind consumed by one thought. "Why?" he muttered. "Twenty men. For what?"

Rankov laid a hamlike hand on the Czech's shoulder. "For the good of communism, comrade, for the salvation of the Eastern bloc, and for the Death Dealer. And, there are times when I am not at all certain which deserves the greater loyalty."

The hand dropped and Rankov turned, plodding back toward the waiting car above them. The Czech followed, his mind still struggling over the waste below. It took a moment, but the Czech let his confusion and loss build into enough of a boil to give him the courage he needed. He gripped Rankov's suitcoat, turning the man from State Security to face him, and greeting his stare with defiance.

"Why didn't you warn me? I could have sent more men. I could have prevented the defection and silenced this agent you call Mercury. Why did you allow those men to be slaughtered?"

Rankov's face iced over, his eyes narrowing into twin laserlike slits as his hand brushed the Czech's hands aside. "There are things in this world greater than your indignation, comrade. It was the Dealer's command that the dogs make good their escape, and it was my job to see that it succeeded. I make it a point not to question the wishes of my superiors, especially those of the Dealer. I have done as I was instructed, and I will now go back to Moscow—to my tiny desk and my immense wife. On both accounts, I suggest you do the same. If not, I am sure you are free to accompany me, courtesy of the State, to lodge your complaints formally. It is my understanding that Lubyanka has many reservations available at this time."

The Czech paled. His courage shredded and oozed out from his body in cold beads of sweat. "But . . . why?" he whispered.

Rankov softened somewhat and stared back toward the battlefield behind them. "There are plans," he said, almost reverently. "I am a servant. I do not know the details. But the Dealer does. They are his plans. And they are big plans, my friend. Immense."

Rankov turned back to the soldier, his hand once more gripping the man's shoulder. "Much bigger than you or I," he sighed. "Much bigger than twenty lives. I do know this. There is an air about Moscow these past few days, a crackling of excitement. There are smiles in the halls of

the Kremlin—and that bodes well for both of us. Come.
There is vodka waiting in the car. Join me in a toast, yes?
To the Dealer and his plans?''

The Czech shuddered as he followed Rankov to the
waiting car. What could be so important about the escape
of a handful of miserable refugees that the Dealer would
ensure their flight by sacrificing twenty lives?

But then, he thought, who was he? Who was anyone to
question the Dealer's motives?

CHAPTER TWO

WASHINGTON, D.C.

Nick stared out the window of the limo as the landscape slipped by. There was a haunted feeling in his brain and a gnawing in his gut that even vehicle-supplied Scotch could not dispel. It had been roughly forty hours since the defection at the Czech border, and yet he still felt as though he were sitting in rural Bohemia.

There was the fog; granted, it was an early morning fog, a mist of rising air drifting off the Potomac. There was granite, man-made monuments of stone that comprised the cemetery of Arlington. There were hills, hummocks, really, mere reminders of the Appalachian chain that dwelt in the west.

But to Nick, it was Bohemia, and the ghosts that had followed him there—the ghosts that should so rightfully have fallen beside the Czech militiamen—were still with him. A mission, so loaded with the potential for resolving the past, had turned out to be an irritant, a reincarnation of doubt and hate.

And Nick could not put his finger on why.

He retreated from the visual reminders of the Arlington landscape, settling back into the leather comfort of the seat, and allowing his thoughts to travel the tufted roof of the passenger compartment.

Part of it was definitely Stefan Borczak, the youthful artist he had once been forced to desert. The man had spent the entire trip back to the United States in silent contemplation. Any attempts on Nick's part to resolve that moment of history had met only with cool politeness and dismissal, attitudes that implied a hint of blame. Mercury would always have his share of credit in the man's loss of sight.

And there was the defection itself. Another routine operation, suddenly glorified with opposition. So like the Berlin affair—so like the Death Dealer. There was almost a signature to it, except that Nick had won. And something about that called for explanation. Anyone can hit a slump, evil geniuses included. But with the Dealer, slumps meant singles instead of homers—never a strike-out.

And the Czech affair had been a strikeout for the Dealer from the first pitch.

But there were no resolutions. Nick could only stare at the Scotch in his hands and let his thoughts swirl right along with the amber liquid. He was so absorbed that he didn't even feel the car drift to a halt. It wasn't until the chauffeur, a brawling bear of a man, pulled open the door and stared at him, his eyes registering firm disapproval of Nick's breakfast habits, that the spell removed itself. With a quick toast toward the driver, Nick downed the remaining Scotch, dropped the glass into his arm-side niche, and pulled himself from the vehicle.

"Count your blessings," he muttered, as much for his own benefit as the chauffeur's.

If the man heard, he gave no indication. His only

response was to guide Nick, with a tilt of his head, toward a thick grouping of people in the near distance. Nick nodded and stepped off toward the gathering of mourners. His tread was silent, as if his feet refused to intrude on the solemnity of the funeral. The only giveaway to his approach was the dark markings his shoes left in the dewy grass beneath.

He searched the ensemble and quickly spotted the shocking mane of white hair and the hunched body of David Hawk.

Hawk was head of AXE, the mastermind and caretaker of one of the most super-secret intelligence organizations ever created. What AXE lacked in notoriety, it more than made up for in effectiveness. Hawk was the daddy and Nick Carter one of his offspring.

Killmaster, N3!

Nick found the man hovering alone, off to the right of the group. Even in his isolation there was a sense of invisibility. His gray overcoat seemed to blend in perfectly with the misting fog of the cemetery, his white hair, a mere crack of sunlight bursting through the haze.

Nick approached softly and settled in beside Hawk, his own hands knotting together in imitation of the mourning stance of the crowd.

There was a brief exchange of glances that told Nick nothing would begin until the service was ended.

Five minutes passed, and then the burial was over. The crowd moved off. Hawk remained standing, slowly pulling cigar and matches from an inside pocket. He lit up, carefully folding cellophane and spent match back into his coat pocket. It was a gesture that spoke far more of years of intelligence work than it ever would of littering national monuments.

He savored his first puff before speaking. "Congratulations. I understand the Czech crossing drew quite an audience."

"A few," Nick shrugged. "Not exactly a full house."

"Good job, nonetheless. I trust the ride up from debrief was to your liking?"

Nick smiled. "It isn't every day you get to ride in the boss's own limo. Thanks."

"You deserved it." The cigar suddenly stabbed out into the air, gesturing off to Nick's left. "Someone else wants to thank you, too. I thought this would be as good a time as any."

Nick turned. Nearing them were three individuals. Nick recognized the man in the center; Representative Karl Ganicek, chairman of the Congressional Committee on Foreign Affairs. The two with him were strangers, but it didn't take a trained eye to spot Secret Service written all over them.

Nick ran the man's bio through his mental computer. Ganicek was one of two sons born to Polish-American parents. With the re-establishment of Poland at the end of World War I, the family moved there to help with the reconstruction. Ganicek's father had climbed the political ladder quite quickly, a rise that was cut brutally short by the Nazi invasion.

The family then fled to England, joining the government in exile, and waiting to see if the Allied powers could save their state. But with the war progressing and England itself under attack, Ganicek's father finally conceded defeat and returned to the United States. Only Ganicek's brother remained to carry on the fight. He joined Military Intelligence in England and was eventually dropped into Poland. He was never heard from again.

After Pearl Harbor, Ganicek joined the U.S. war effort, drawing duty as language specialist for the forces advancing toward central Europe. It was his hope to be involved when the Allies freed his native country, but the Russians took the honors instead. After the war, Ganicek entered Poland. He spent three years trying to get involved in the postwar machinery and trying to track down his brother. Both projects were frustrated at every turn.

With the Soviet strategy of ''liberation'' becoming evident to all, Ganicek finally gave up his struggle. He returned to the United States and spent several years, as he put it, ''brooding over events I could not control.'' It took a car accident in the fifties—an accident that claimed the lives of both his parents, and very nearly his own—to finally shake him from his personal defeat.

Ganicek wanted a voice in European affairs, and he went for it. He ran for Congress, riding the anti-Communist tide of the fifties, and got elected. He made good his commitments, remaining, even after the deterioration of McCarthyism, a staunch anti-Soviet presence in Congress. He was also recognized as a master of Foreign Affairs legislation. He was now well into his seventh term, a Democratic hammer whose weight could always be counted on—even by Republican regimes—whenever it came to questions of Soviet policy.

Physically, Ganicek was anything but awesome, five feet nine, a compacted cyclone of pure determination. He had lightly Slavic features, slender but rounded, with a thin stream of white hair that raced back from a balding skull. His entire face seemed to pinch inward toward his wire-rimmed spectacles.

In an era of television campaigners, he was anything but photogenic. The deep scars of his accident cut through his face like a road map. But his constituents could obviously care less. To them, the scars were only reminders of how deep his commitments lay.

Nick nodded in greeting as the man approached him. It was a hand with a grip of iron that captured his own.

''This is perhaps not the best time,'' came the resonant voice. ''But I just wanted to say thank you for what you have done.''

Nick shrugged, giving him a brief smile as the man

pumped his hand. What, on the surface, appeared to be
abject humility, was in reality Nick's invitation for Hawk
to take the conversational lead. AXE was known to only a
few individuals, and Nick was not about to be the first to
let it slip.

Hawk took the lead. "This is Mercury, Mr. Congressman. I think you'll understand if we don't identify
him further."

"Of course," Ganicek nodded. "I don't need details. It
is enough to know that you have been responsible for
freeing several of my countrymen. The President tells me
that this is not the first time you've accomplished such a
mission. I just wanted to thank you personally. As someone who's lived there, I wanted you to know just how
much your actions have meant. You're a credit to the CIA
and a hero to any who value human rights."

"It's my job," Nick answered, and then grinned. "But
a little recognition never hurts. I'll remember your
thoughts next time, sir. I appreciate your speaking to
me."

The congressman beamed his approval. "Good luck,
young man. I know you must be tired, so I won't take up
any more of your time." He tossed a wave toward Hawk
and departed, his watchdogs dutifully following. Nick
and Hawk let the others move off before turning and
drifting toward the waiting limo.

"Why the kudos?" Nick asked. "You don't usually go
for that much exposure."

Hawk pulled the cigar from between clenched teeth and
heaved a thick column of smoke into the morning air.
"The President hinted that he would be very appreciative
if I were to bend the rules just a bit, at least where Ganicek
is concerned."

"Any particular reason?"

Hawk nodded. "How well have you been following the
upcoming Bern convention?"

Nick gave a quick chuckle. "You don't have to follow it, Hawk. It follows you."

The Bern Conference on International Human Rights was the story of the decade. Though still two weeks away, it was accumulating more press coverage than any event Nick could remember. It was the President's own personal brainchild, and, for a man accused of inexperience in foreign affairs, it was something of a coup d'état—personally and politically.

Its claim was to out-Helsinki the Helsinki Accords, and to make good that claim, the President had committed himself to personally attending each of the conference's six major sessions. Most of the previous presidential year had been spent in back-room negotiations, all designed to see that allied leaders matched the President with equal or nearly equal commitment. And so far the responses had been astounding.

"The old man has quite a show going," chortled Hawk.

"Now," Nick added, "if he could only get the Communist countries to join him, he'd have re-election in his hip pocket."

There was a quick stab from Hawk's wary eyes, a chastising look that implied ill of the uninformed agent. Just as quickly came a forgiving dismissal of the glance. "I forget," Hawk grumbled. "You've been a bit out of touch for the last few days."

Nick's brow furrowed questioningly. "You mean the Iron Curtain has joined the parade of dignitaries?"

"Joined!" Hawk roared. "You'd think the Premier had his own re-election at stake! He dropped his blockbuster in Moscow last night, and it's consuming the front page of every tabloid in America Not only is he *personally* seeing the President, but he's raising him two or three."

"You mean he'll show up himself?"

"Indeed," Hawk nodded. "And he's bringing a few of

the Politburo's more prestigious octogenarians with
him.''

"And just where does Ganicek fit into all this?"

"Well, regardless of party affiliation, there's always
one thing any President can count on from Congressman
Ganicek, and that's a hard-line Soviet position, a position
the current regime feels quite at home with. Whatever
other issues they may differ on, the President and Ganicek
seem to have made a small marriage vis à vis the Red
menace.''

Nick once more picked up the thread. "And nothing
would increase the President's bargaining power more
than a united front at the Bern negotiations—the Allies
tucked in one holster, his political opposition at home in
the other.''

"Exactly,'' Hawk nodded, his eyes bright with approval. "Ganicek will attend the conference as the President's number one negotiator. And he's more than a
holster-full, N3. He's double-barreled. He represents a
bipartisan front on the one hand, and a living record of
Soviet abuses on the other. I pity the poor negotiator that
has to look Ganicek in the face, and then speak of the joys
of Soviet life.''

"Is that why the President wanted him to meet me? A
little shot to get the juices flowing?''

"No doubt.''

The driver held the limo door open as the two men
approached, then closed it softly behind them and moved
around to his position behind the wheel. The car eased off
into the morning mists.

"Only one thing I don't get,'' Nick mused as the car
picked up speed and pulled out onto the parkway. "If the
President is going into the Bern conference so well armed,
why are the Soviets so ready to go under the gun? They've
got the occupation of Afghanistan, yellow rain in South-
east Asia—any number of reasons for backing out. Instead, they're walking in with bells on. Why?''

Hawk digested the question for a few seconds, sliding his window down and watching as the smoke from his cigar curled out. Finally he answered, his voice somewhat distant and unsure.

"On the surface, it would all appear somewhat masochistic, I grant you. But, if what your Polish artist friend has been telling us is true, the picture gets very ugly."

"Borczak?" Nick squawked.

Hawk nodded. "The President is going over the debrief now. He should make some kind of decision within the next hour or so. Until then, I'd rather not get into too much speculation."

And then Hawk turned and looked at Nick sharply. "But if Borczak's claims do hold water, we'll be operational by this afternoon. The Dealer is involved, Nick—up to his ugly ears. And if we're going to move, I want you handling the whole show."

Nick's eyes grew hard and icy. "If the Dealer's involved, it would be pretty hard to keep me away from it."

Hawk smiled, his teeth clamping down on the cigar. "I thought you might feel that way. So, since we've got a few hours to kill, how does breakfast sound?"

"You buying?"

Hawk nodded with a chuckle.

"Then you've got a date," Nick replied, turning his gaze out the window to the Virginia countryside. "By the way. Who did we just put to rest?"

"You *have* been out of touch," Hawk grunted, shaking his head. "Representative Harris, Speaker of the House. Stroke. The papers have been full of it."

Nick whistled. "I didn't think he was that old."

"He wasn't," Hawk growled. "It was very sudden and very unexpected." Here the big man sighed and ran the fingers of his free hand across his forehead in a gesture of resignation. "It's modern times, I guess. The stress and strain of the computerized nuclear age."

Nick grinned. "It's nice you and I have our nice cushy jobs without the strain of big government or big business."

"You dodge bullets, I dodge budgets," Hawk chuckled. "But I wouldn't have it any other way."

Nick nodded. "Who will be Harris' successor?"

Hawk gave a noncommittal shrug. "If you listen to the press, there are a couple of old-boy regulars ready to don the mantle. But, if you listen to the echoes in the trenches, Ganicek's name keeps popping up."

"One more bit of ammunition for the conference?"

"I would say so," Hawk nodded. "The vote comes up today."

"Any bets on which way it'll go?"

"I don't gamble, N3. Surely you know that," Hawk replied, his voice a hard rumble in his chest. "Betting is a commitment made on the unknowable. I like certainty. I collect tiny little pieces and then patch them into bigger pictures. When the picture is clear, then I'll commit."

"And what's the picture on this afternoon's vote?"

"Ganicek," Hawk said flatly. Then he turned to Nick, his eyes twinkling mischievously. "Bet on it."

The man stood staring out the window, his hands clutched limply behind his back. The sun was breaking through the fog, turning what had been a dismal morning into a brilliant festival of spring light. Shadows were breaking across the long lawn, pointing their way to the surrounding iron fencework. There was even the faintest hint of lilac fragrance, somehow managing to find its way through bulletproof glass to tease at the man's nostrils.

But none of it was powerful enough to dissuade the man's mood. Inside, he was fog, and dead trees, and winter, all in one. He turned from the window, his movement punctuated with another sigh, and surveyed the interior of his world. The Oval Office, the goal of so many ambitious men, seemed this day no more than a tomb.

...houghts assailed him, quotes that spoke of impossibilities, of an office "too unwieldy to be managed by any one man," of responsibilities "too great to be individually borne."

And it was only—what?—five, six hours ago, he was toasting his fate, raising his orange juice high, joking with the aides that had torn him from his bed. "Where's the vodka?" he had jested. "What's orange juice without vodka? It's called a screwdriver, folks. And you know why? Because when the Soviets get to Bern, we'll be doing the driving, and—well—I'll let you figure out what they'll be getting."

So much responsive laughter. A year's worth of work, a year of handing out plums, to allies, to opposition party members, all to create this one singular event. Bern. And now, chaos.

The man walked over to his desk, his eyes riveted on the thin brief that occupied the center. It was only paper, but to the man who occupied the Oval Office, it was a death warrant. One dissident slips through the Iron Curtain, and he brings with him the end of a dream.

The man lifted the brief, his eyes scanning for the hundredth time the typewritten words that had authored his mood.

No, dammit!

The papers slammed back onto the desk. Nothing was going to stop the conference. Not even this—this Dealer, whoever the hell he was. Nothing would stand in the way of Bern. There was a Presidential reputation at stake, true. There was maybe even just a touch of ego, a touch of politics. But most importantly, there were millions of damned souls buried under the yoke of tyranny and torture and arbitrary imprisonment; there *was* a question of human dignity at stake.

The man plopped himself into the high-backed chair, ignoring the loud squeals of leather. He swept the brief to his right, a firm gesture that spoke of defiance, while his other hand leafed through a series of computer cards, cards that allowed him direct connections to certain individuals, individuals that even his secretary was unaware of.

He popped in a card and waited patiently for the call to be answered.

There were games to be played, and there was only one man that the President felt secure in playing with.

The rings gave way to a computerized hum, a sound that indicated the call was being transferred to remote. The man might be out of his office, but he could be reached, anytime, anywhere.

There was another sequence of dull bursting electronics, and then, finally, a voice. "Yes?"

"David," said the man, "I need to see you. Right away."

"Just finishing breakfast," Hawk replied, with just the right tone of respect in his voice. "I'll be right there, sir."

The man occupying the Oval Office was not the only one filled with intense emotion this spring day. There were others, aides, men close to the President, whose futures would be determined by the decisions made within the next few hours. One such aide was feeling his own fair share of depression.

Jacek Januslawski paced his office, his desk occupied by a single brief. Unlike the man in the Oval Office, this brief held little of his attention. It represented an unofficial probe, an informal tally of votes that seemed to indicate that Karl Ganicek would be the next Speaker of the House of Representatives.

It was the kind of news that should have led to celebration. "Vodka!" Jacek might have once cried. But, of course, *that* was a luxury that thirteen years of spying had erased. Still, a celebration of some sort should have been in the offing. It is rare when any mole finds himself so elevated in the superstructure of an opposing government.

But Jacek was anything but joyous.

He walked to the window of his office, and, like the man just a few blocks away, he studied the sunny landscape. Below him was the sprawl of Washington traffic, ebbing its way down the streets that surrounded the Congressional Office Building. Like the aide watching it, it was a study in known goals going sour in the face of congested reality.

It had all seemed so simple just thirteen years ago. One studies, one trains, one spends precious years refining skills— training to betray *any* and *all* for the cause. And then, one ventures out, digging into the intestines of the enemy, setting oneself up as a pipeline of information. And not once, not ever, does guilt rear its head.

Until now.

But why now?

Part of it was Ganicek. The man who offered so much. The man who had lived under the aegis of the Soviet giant, and said "No!" The man who had read of the defector, read of the story at the Berlin Wall and said, "Let me be the first to welcome you, with appreciation, with relief, and with a job."

That was part of it, no doubt. Ganicek was climbing, and that meant that Jacek would climb with him. More prestige, more responsibility, and more information flowing back in greater bits of betrayal. But that could be lived with. That was no more than Jacek expected when he took on the role of agent.

Some of it was Borczak, too—the artist, the friend. The one man Jacek found it worth standing up for, even to the likes of the Dealer. "He must not die," Jacek had said. "He must accompany me on the defection. If he doesn't, suspicions may arise. But he must not share the fate of the scientists. He *must* live! I want your promise on that."

And the boy did survive. But now Jacek had the rumors to taunt him. "There's been a defection," said the gossip mongers. "Couldn't be better timed . . . Bern, and all.

It's an artist. Borjack, or something like that. They blinded the poor son-of-a-bitch. Can you believe it? God, we should nuke the bastards and never look back.''

Stefan had lived, and survived, and had worked himself out of the Soviet grip. For that Jacek felt relief. But with dead eyes there would be no Tiergarten, no buxom women, only hate, and depression, and the agony of thirteen years of sightless confusion.

For that, Jacek felt remorse.

But that wasn't all of it. Just Stefan's sightless eyes wasn't what now tore at Jacek's insides and made him pace his office floor like a caged tiger with sweaty palms and a brooding scowl on his face.

It was also what they were now asking him to do. In the beginning it wasn't in the game plan. Not once, in the entire course of his KGB training, did they tell him that he would ever be asked to kill.

And now they had.

At least, that was the assumption Jacek had to draw from what had occurred. The lighter had been handed to him—as had every other instruction—through Ikon, the man at the Soviet Embassy who gave Rasputin all his instructions. There had been the usual meeting, Harper's Ferry, the deviation from the tour route, the treehouse, two hundred meters from the road. All, just as it had been every other time.

But this time there was the lighter, and the vial. The lighter had stabbed his finger, and the vial had never been explained. All he had been told was to fill the lighter from the small ampule of liquid, and then drop it at the appointed desk. ''Congressman Ganicek wishes to express his thanks,'' was all he was told to say.

Murder, any way you cut it. And that was one thing they had never prepared him for.

Jacek's thoughts were interrupted by an explosion of sound as Congressman Ganicek roared through the door. ''How does it look, Jacek?''

The spy took a moment to compose himself, aware that his attitude was one of defeat. He let the question dangle, building his cover—as he was trained to do—turning the moment of introspective doubt into one of friendly teasing. "I'm sorry to say, sir, that if all the calculations are correct . . . ." Jacek then turned from the window, ". . . you will be confirmed as Speaker."

Ganicek's eyes narrowed, then lit up with appreciation. He answered his aide's jest with appropriate restraint. "Thank you, Jacek." Then, with a humor of his own, he added, "I think you've just earned yourself a day off."

Ganicek turned back toward his own office, his progress halted by the sound of Jacek's voice. "I'll make you a trade, sir."

The congressman turned back to face him. "Oh?"

"I understand there's a Stefan Borczak who has defected. I—I think I knew him. If possible, I would like to meet him—just to be sure. If it's the same man, we were very close—at least *then*."

A look of interest crossed the congressman's face. "Of course, Jacek. There has indeed been a defector—an artist, I understand, named Stefan Borczak. Could that be the same one?"

Jacek nodded.

"I will see what I can do," Ganicek answered with a smile. "For the moment, he is under tight security. You can understand that, I'm sure."

"Of course. But it is very important to me . . ."

Ganicek stared, and then stepped over to embrace Jacek's arm. "I don't suppose it would hurt if I were to ask the President. It's quite possible an exemption might be made in your case. After all," he grinned, his eyes lighting up with a conspiratorial twinkle, "the old boy needs all the votes he can get. If I succeed, does that mean I have re-earned your services for the day?"

"Yes, sir. Most willingly."

"Good!" the congressman beamed. "Now, do you

have the Soviet data I asked you to compile?''

Jacek nodded.

''Then let's get to work. We have a lot to do before Bern!''

With that, the man departed.

CHAPTER THREE

Nick stood patiently in the elevator, allowing the crowd to file out and empty the compartment. This was the fifth floor of Amalgamated Press and Wire Services, Dupont Circle headquarters. It was quite legitimate; the departing chatter of the elevator's occupants was indication enough of that. There were shared bits of storyline, news breaks in the making, and hints of tomorrow's headlines—with, by far, the greatest lip service being offered to the upcoming Bern affair.

Nick waited for the doors to close, leaving him alone in the elevator. He then reached up to the selection panel and popped open the tiny door marked "Danger—High Voltage." Beneath the door was a tiny computer scanner screen and a voice register, Nick's key to the upper floors that housed the *real* purpose behind Amalgamated Press.

AXE.

Nick coded in the proper number sequence on the floor selection panel, and then held his palm up to the scanner. There was a faint hum of electronics and a rapid green flash beneath his hand as the scanner toured his palm, satisfying the complex machinery beyond.

Then came three sharp beeps.

"Code 2271-24," Nick intoned. "Classification N3, priority A21-874-KMR."

He dropped his hand away as the panel confirmed his message, verifying in green LED print across the screen that voice and hand scans were in order. It then repeated the coding sequence back, asking politely if the entry was correct. Nick confirmed the entry, and then settled back as the elevator gave a gentle lift toward the sixth—and most sacrosanct—floor of the building.

Nick reached into his pocket and withdrew one of his gold-tipped cigarettes from its case. It was a gesture born partially of a desire for a smoke, and partially for self-defense. Any visit to Hawk's office was a descent into a smoke-filled abyss created by the man's cigar. Although not as pungent, Nick's own Turkish blend of tobacco offered at least minor defense.

But as Nick lit up, it was not the comparative merits of tobaccos that was consuming his thoughts; it was the Death Dealer. He had just spent the better part of the day, each moment since he had parted from Hawk, digging into the archives, pulling and reading every file that might contain any mention of the man he was about to go up against.

Nick had come to the conclusion that he was truly an enigma; an amazing enigma. Rather than no name, the man had several, all aliases, and all discarded for a new one when the old one became well known.

There were only vague descriptions of his physical appearance, and hardly any information on his background. Possible places of birth ranged from Georgia to the Ukraine to Moscow itself. It was as if he had emerged full-blown and full-grown from the bowels of KGB headquarters in Dzerzhinsky Square.

In this modern day and age it was almost impossible for a man to circulate the way the Dealer had and not build up some kind of dossier in at least one espionage service besides his own. Somehow the Dealer had done just that, remaining a mystery to even his own henchmen.

But still Nick had dug out whatever information he could, preparing himself, loading the computerlike circuitry of his brain, immersing himself in every detail of the man's methods, and thought, and execution. When they met this time, the Dealer was not going to walk away.

Nick could feel the tingling sensations of finality coursing through him. There would be no next time. Not anymore.

The door slid silently open and Nick stepped out into the somber dignity of the AXE nerve center. He turned left, moving across deep-piled burgundy carpeting, past closed doors with other scanners for knobs and other voice registers for keys, seeking out the office of the man who ran the show.

He stepped up to the door slowly, allowing the overhead camera to announce his presence. There was a second's delay, and then the soft click of bolts releasing. Nick pushed on the oaken door and moved into the inner sanctum.

He was promptly greeted by the sight of a delightful derriere bent over a desk.

"Ah, Bateman," Nick grinned, "you get lovelier every day." The door clicked shut behind him.

Before him, the figure rose slowly, turning to greet him with eyes sparkling with sarcasm. Ginger Bateman would be lovely wearing any emotion, but anger somehow always fit her best. There was something about those flashing green eyes, the flaming red hair, and the subtle sophistication of her southern accent that made bantering an almost sexual experience.

"Carter," she oozed, "you have a one-track mind. Not a fault in itself, mind you, but somewhere along the line I just can't help but think it derailed."

With a bright flash of a smile, she scooped up the files on her desk and slithered over to the open drawer of the cabinet. Nick watched the move with admiration. It was a ballet of limbs and motion, a test of the holding power of synthetic fabric.

"You know, Bateman, one of these days you're going to succumb to my charms. It's inevitable—like death and taxes," he grinned.

Ginger paused in her filing, her eyes darting impishly toward the ceiling, her tongue curling thoughtfully over rich, thick, ruby lips. "Death and taxes, huh?" With a quick sigh, she shrugged. "Sorry, y'all. It just sounds like too dull an evening, and much too expensive."

Nick's laughter filled the room, accompanied by Ginger's smile. Both were interrupted by the crackling of the intercom. "N3," came the somber drone, "if you are through molesting the help, there are matters that need your attention."

Nick coughed out a quick, "Yes, sir," and, with a quick wink to Ginger, moved through the door.

Hawk's office was just as it ever was, a monument of leather and mahogany, a simple, elegant statement of functional furnishings, filled with various mementos of Hawk's career. Hawk sat behind his massive desk, the air around him surprisingly clear and devoid of the usual swirling of omnipresent cigar smoke. With a nod in his direction, Nick stopped short, his hand still on the doorknob.

He and Hawk were definitely not alone in the room.

To his left was the sofa, its occupants quite familiar. Stefan Borczak was sitting forward on the seat, his hands resting atop his cane, his eyes drifting in Nick's general direction. Beside him was his wife, Hela. For a moment her eyes met Nick's; then just as quickly they dropped to the floor. Nick watched her a moment. What had been a beautiful face when encountered during the defection, was now, if possible, even more beautiful. AXE had done its best to make the newcomers feel welcome. There were just the subtlest indications of makeup and the calm settling of facial features that said years of secrets and tension were over.

Nick then glanced to his right. There were two chairs with a side table between them. Both were occupied. One contained Albert Rackley, the Presidential aide that served as liaison to intelligence affairs, the man who made sure what it was that the President did—or did not—want to know about AXE activities. In the other chair was a lady that Nick had not seen for years. She met his eyes and held them, and a smile tugged at the corners of her mouth. Nick remembered that smile. It was like the rest of her— well formed and sensuous, without being glaringly sexual.

Tori Bacchus: designation, Killmaster N20.

Nick returned the smile. Tori was a top-notch agent, a woman with whom he had shared several missions. Her station had been the Middle East, and there were at least three times that Nick could recall where her skill and expertise had saved the day. Although their relationship had never transcended the professional, that had always been more a result of circumstance than desire.

Nick acknowledged the lady with a nod, her own lustrous brown hair bowing in response. He then turned to Hawk. The man was waiting patiently for the preliminaries to end. He gestured toward the chair to the left of his desk.

"Good afternoon, N3. Sit. We have a lot to discuss. And would you be so kind as to put out your cigarette? Mr. Rackley has asked that there be no smoking."

Nick took the chair and stubbed out the remainder of his cigarette. Somehow, Rackley was never a welcome addition to the proceedings.

"Thank you, N3," Hawk nodded, and then addressed the room. "I'm sure you are all familiar enough with each other. I think we should get on with what needs to be said. I don't mean to appear abrupt, but the information that Mr. Borczak has given us is somewhat frightening in its proportions. There are decisions that need to be made here today, and those decisions will have a phenomenal impact on the upcoming Bern negotiations—an event you are all familiar enough with to understand without any added introduction.''

Hawk turned to the Polish artist and his wife and continued. ''Mr. Borczak,'' he said, his body settling back into his chair, ''if you would start, please? Tell the others here exactly what it was you told the agents at debrief.''

The dissident moved himself to the edge of the sofa, his hands grinding away at the carved fist of his cane handle. His wife's eyes remained glued to the floor. ''Perhaps some background? At least for Merc—Mr. Carter's sake?''

''Yes,'' Hawk nodded. ''It would be good for all to hear.''

Nick shifted in his chair until he could face Borczak directly.

''First of all,'' said the artist, his sightless eyes remaining neutrally pointed on the far wall, ''I owe you something of an apology. My behavior since the defection has been—what—distant, shall we say? It has occurred to me—''

His voice suddenly stopped, his hand moving over to touch his wife's knee. She responded by lifting her gaze from the floor and staring at the man. ''Let's be accurate, shall we?'' he continued. ''My wife has made it clear that perhaps I have been less than grateful for what you did, Mr. Carter. My treatment of you, on the return flight and at the debriefings, has been less than cordial. For that, you have my deepest apology.''

Nick shrugged. ''Accepted, but unnecessary. Berlin was an incident both of us have had to live with—you more than I. I have never forgotten it and trust that I'll never again have to make a similar choice. I ask you to forgive what had to be.''

The man smiled. "It is more important to dwell on what that event has yielded, yes?"

"I think so," Nick answered.

"I quite agree," Borczak nodded. "Now, since that time several things have occurred. Briefly, I was taken by the Dealer, and blinded. That event was not an arbitrary one, and it was extremely effective in terms of my commitments to Polish freedom. The Dealer knew his man. With my sight removed, I lost all desire to fight for anything. I—surrendered to reality."

Nick's eyes flickered around the room. No one seemed able to meet the dead eyes of the speaker. He was confessing, and that made them uncomfortable. Borczak seemed to sense it.

"What this means to all of you," he continued, "is that I accepted the Dealer's will. I suppose the man was generous, at least in his own terms. He took my sight, but did not turn me out. Instead, he put me to work—in his own office."

That bit of information immediately got everyone's attention. There was an audible gasp from Tori Bacchus, and Rackley leaned forward intently in his chair.

Borczak smiled and nodded. "I thought that would interest you. The Dealer is a very cautious and secretive man, even within his own organization. He has a system, one that has to be admired. It is his habit to surround himself with those who cannot see; his files are kept in Braille. It is a system designed to accommodate the greatest of security. There can be no betrayal. There are no documents that can be photographed. There is only a small group of blind men, punching out records, records laid down from verbal sessions with the Dealer himself."

Borczak turned once more, sightless eyes leaning toward the woman to his left, his hand touching the knee beside him. "There was even the question of companionship, again taken care of by the Dealer himself. Women

were ordered to mate with the blind men upon whom the
Dealer's security depended.'' His voice became very low.
"It was not the most pleasant of assignments, and not all
of the women took to their tasks with the dedication that
Hela has. For that, there can never be enough gratitude—
or enough love.''

The woman removed her gaze from her husband, her
own eyes returning to the floor, her face a hard mask that
Nick could not penetrate. Respect, Nick could read, even
admiration. But the word *love* seemed to drive the lady's
eyes deep into the carpeting.

Borczak's hand rose from her knee and settled back
onto the cane. "But that has little to do with these proceedings. What does affect you is this: I accepted my defeat, at
least until about a year ago. It was then, through the good
promptings of my wife, that I became aware of the events
blossoming at Bern. It was through her interest in the
hopeful results of the conference that I began to make
certain discoveries. As time moved on, it became clear
that, while Hela was seeing the conference in one light,
the Dealer was seeing it in quite another. More and more
office time was being consumed with this conference, and
its results had little similarity to the discussions I was
having at home.''

He paused, a small smile playing at the corners of his
mouth. "Once I was able to sense the events,'' he continued, "I found certain animosities rekindled within me.
I rediscovered the will to fight. With Hela's support, I
found the courage to attack the Dealer's files.''

Albert Rackley's eyebrow shot up. "Just how is it you
were able to accomplish that?''

A low chuckle rumbled from Borczak's chest. "A good
question, my friend. The Dealer is a very thorough man;
his system is quite sophisticated. He ran his sessions with
us on a rotation basis. Whenever anything needed to be
recorded, we would be summoned individually. All re-
ports were delivered verbally, each man taking the as-

signment by virtue of his position in the rotation. In this
way, he was able to keep any one of us from ever getting a
complete picture. *But*—it is a system designed to protect
from the *outside*. The Dealer never anticipated activity
from within. Broken and blinded men do not fight, gentlemen, I can assure you from experience.''

''So how is it you were able to accumulate your data?''
Rackley persisted.

''I went about my duties, as ever, but whenever the
Dealer was out of the office, I would spend greater
amounts of time at the files. I would enter my own work,
but take advantage of my access to read the entries of the
others. Who was there to stop me? The blind may lead the
blind, but they can never catch them.''

Rackley nodded his satisfaction as Hawk leaned forward intently over his desk. ''So you were able to gather
the data. What did you do then?''

''I created my own file—'' Borczak's right hand came
up to tap his brow ''—here! And when I felt the picture
was as complete as it ever would be, I began to plan my
escape, using the Dealer's own channels, I might add. I
asked for Mercury, invoking a name from the past, and the
rest you all know.''

There was a general stirring in the room as everyone
digested the information they had just heard. Then Hawk
leaned forward once more.

''What we are here to discuss is the plot that Mr.
Borczak has uncovered. It is a plan, authored by the
Dealer, to cripple the conference at Bern.''

''But why?'' Tori Bacchus asked. ''They can do that by
just not showing up. Instead, if the newspapers are accurate, they'll be coming to Bern in force. Why the elaborate
efforts, when they could avoid the conference and pretty
much make a sham out of it.''

Hawk shrugged. ''Partly, it's the old cat-and-mouse
game. They could avoid it, but the Russians are very short
on good public relations these days. An appearance, espe-

cially in the face of such delicate issues, would give them quite a boost. More accurately, though, it's a matter of solid politics—*internal* politics. The Premier is new to the top job, and he must still consolidate his power within the Politburo. If what Mr. Borczak has told us is accurate, the Dealer has given him one hell of an attention-getting stroke.''

''For the Premier *and* himself,'' Borczak interjected, and then turned in Nick's direction. ''Do you remember your encounter with the Dealer in Berlin, Mr. Carter?''

''I could hardly forget it,'' Nick replied, his voice like stone.

''Just so,'' Borczak nodded. ''But in Berlin, Mr. Carter, he was young, and climbing. Since Berlin, events have been kind to him. Thanks to you, his efforts in Germany came to an end, but something occurred that night that affected him. I can only attribute it to you, Mercury. You gave him a new name. The Death Dealer, you called him—and he seemed to take to it with abandon. From that moment on, assassination became his trade. He climbed the hierarchy of the KGB using this as his method. The leaders above him could not remain blind to such effectiveness. The Director nurtured the Death Dealer, growing ever more fond of the results he could create.''

His cane lifted to stab the air. ''Now, with the ascension of the Dealer's old mentor from chief of the KGB to Premier of all the Soviet Union, the Dealer sees even a brighter political future for himself. He sees it as a future with more power and an even vaster scope for his unique talents! For now, he is dedicating more of his efforts to the man who once led him than to the country he claims to serve. But it is ultimately the Dealer he serves. Never forget that! Never!''

Hawk stood and moved from behind his desk. ''What we have, ladies and gentlemen, is a dilemma. What we

also have, thanks to Mr. Borczak and his wife, is knowledge of that dilemma. The Dealer has used both his own
and the Premier's experience in intelligence affairs to
create a dossier. Details of the dossier are sketchy—it
wasn't the kind of information the Dealer shared with his
staff. But enough of it was discussed or referred to for Mr.
Borczak to at least give us a clue of its scope."

"How bad is it?" Tori asked.

Hawk eased his bulk onto the edge of the desk and
folded his arms across his chest. "As far as we can
determine, nothing too outrageous. But then, it doesn't
have to be. It is presentation, rather than content, that
makes this situation unique. In the first place, you have a
Soviet Premier with firm intelligence connections behind
him, years of intimate, firsthand contact with the events.
This in its own right will carry a certain power."

He heaved a thoughtful sigh and moved to stare out the
window behind his desk. "Beyond that," he continued,
"the Dealer has arranged a little show, one that will add
even further impact to the accusations he intends to see
leveled. It seems that we have been harboring a mole in
our midst, one who is scheduled to be at the conference,
and one who intends to defect the instant the Russians
make public their accusations. It is their intent to provide
the world with proof positive of U.S. human rights violations, and then have the mole defect and confirm the
story."

"But it's all a sham!" Rackley thundered, jerking in his
chair. "Surely that will be obvious! Is the dossier really so
damaging? Don't we have information of our own to
throw back at them?"

Hawk turned from the window and raised a hand to
calm the outburst. "The dossier may or may not be
damaging—and, yes, there are no doubt stories we can
toss back. The question, really, is whether or not we can
afford to turn the conference into a slug-fest. Truth or not,

reality or not, the President cannot afford to have the conference break down in verbal battles that will divert events from their true purpose.''

"Do we know the identity of the mole?" Tori asked.

Hawk sighed. "Unfortunately, yes. His name is Jacek Januslawski.''

"What?" Nick roared, instantly coming out of his chair. "Jacek . . .?"

Hawk nodded, and Borczak's voice sounded from behind Nick.

"Yes, Mercury. The one man who made it over the wall that night in Berlin. Even then, it would seem, the Dealer was weaving his webs.''

"You're positive about the identification?" Nick said, turning back to Hawk.

"Absolutely," came the answer. "The Dealer placed his man well. Jacek is the personal aide to Congressman Ganicek, the President's chief negotiator at the conference. We can all imagine the significance of such a highly placed individual, not only defecting in protest over Soviet revelations, but *re*defecting! If you add to this the fact that Congressman Ganicek also serves on the Combined Congressional Committee for Intelligence Oversight, you have an aide with a highly credible access to the very accusations the Soviets intend to make.''

"Well, stop him!" Rackley bellowed. "You know who he is—arrest him! Keep him from showing up at all!''

Hawk looked wearily at the man with the strident voice and the bureaucratic manner. "Mr. Rackley, we don't *want* to.''

Under other circumstances, the astonishment on Rackley's face would have evoked laughter. His mouth dropped and his jaw made vague stabs at speech, but anything approaching sound seemed to lose itself in the saucer-wide eyes. "But—but—" he stuttered.

Hawk's voice became more soothing and tolerant. "If we don't face this now," he said, "it will always be a sword hanging over our heads. Yes, we can arrest Januslawski and keep him from the conference. But then we never really learn what it is the Soviets think they've got. On the other hand, we can proceed. We can allow the Soviets to think they're going to pull it off, but take our own countermeasures. If we can convince them to hit us with their weapons in closed session, we can counter them, gaining both the absolute knowledge of their information, and impressing them with the uselessness of this sort of approach in the future.''

"You can do that?" Rackley asked. There was a naiveté in the question that neither Tori nor Nick could continue to ignore. The first burst of stifled response came from the female agent. There was a choking gasp of air, and then the diligent attempt to wipe the smile from her face. Rackley just turned to her, his eyes a blank desert of incomprehension.

"Yes," Hawk said, his own voice disguising humor. "We think we can. As it stands right now, the Dealer has sold the Premier on his scheme. He has convinced him to match the President in his commitment to the conference, and he has persuaded him to include several of his own rivals in the Soviet delegation. The Dealer himself will be in Bern to run the show. The Premier will get the credit, of course, but the Dealer will gain his own rewards.''

"I still don't understand," Rackley said, honest confusion furrowing his brow.

"If they win," Hawk explained, "the negotiations break down in chaos. The Premier cements his position in the Soviet hierarchy, and the Dealer gains power with him. If they lose, the Premier will suffer a setback, and we discourage any such attempt in the future." He shrugged. "It's a gamble—but one we feel compelled to take.''

"What kind of ammunition do we have to use against them?" Nick asked.

Hawk gestured to where Stefan sat on the couch. "Fortunately, Mr. Borczak departed his country with more than just a plot in his possession. Perhaps he can explain it better.''

The blind man nodded. ''As I mentioned, I gathered information in bits and pieces, and filed it. But there was one project that the Dealer gave to me alone. Why, I'm not sure. Perhaps he felt my allegiance was secure. In any event, this particular project was sort of an insurance policy for the Dealer himself. He is a man very aware of the mechanics of Soviet life. He knows that purges are a part of Russian history that no one ignores. To protect himself from such a purge, he created a cache of personal records that outlined missions and assassination decisions in full detail. He keeps this diary, if you will, outside the borders of Russia, with people he has developed on his own. It is inaccessible to any within the KGB, to any who do not know how—and where—to find it.''

''And you do?'' Rackley chimed. Borczak nodded. ''Well, good! Get it!''

''We intend to,'' Hawk interjected. ''We *will* get it. And we'll shove it down the Russians' throats at the conference. At our convenience, of course. In the meantime, we'll be keeping the Soviet mole under surveillance, and doing all we can to convince the Russians that their plan is still operative.''

This time Tori stepped in. ''With Borczak's defection, won't the Russians back off? The Dealer has to know what the extent of his losses are.''

''I'm not entirely sure he knows I'm gone yet,'' Borczak answered. ''I timed my departure with care. The Dealer was visiting the Premier's dacha outside Moscow for several days of planning. He would only be returning tonight. It is possible he will be searching for me, but I doubt he knows I've reached the West.''

''He knows.'' It was Nick's turn to interrupt. All eyes turned in his direction. ''Two dozen Czech militia don't show up at a defection just for practice. You may have had the run of the office, Stefan, but the country has very watchful eyes to guard it. I promise you, the Dealer knew you were gone within the hour. His involvements with the Premier may have kept him from throwing his usual finesse into stopping you, but he ordered it.''

Borczak sighed, then nodded slowly. "It is possible."

Nick turned to Hawk. "The whole Czech affair has been bothering me. Now I know why. The Dealer tried to stop it; he just couldn't get there to head it off. We're lucky he couldn't. We made it."

Hawk nodded his agreement. "The Dealer may know Stefan is gone, but he doesn't know how much homework he's done, how much information Stefan has given us. As far as he's concerned, Borczak only knew portions of the Bern project. And the setup is too ripe; it's too great an opportunity to get the Premier planted firmly for the Dealer to back out now. The only thing in doubt is his private little 'insurance policy.' ''

"And he's damn sure Stefan knows about that," Nick mumbled, as much to himself as to the others.

A smile creased Borczak's lips. "But he doesn't know that I have unearthed the location of his private diary. Therefore, I doubt that he will move it."

"Unless," Nick added, "he thought we were going after it."

"And that will be a big part of our job," Hawk said, rising and leaning forward across his desk with his weight firmly on his palms. "We must keep him thinking the diary is safe, until we can get to it."

"How do we do that?" Tori asked.

"Well, we've concocted a little plan of our own," Hawk said. "First, we've planned a five-city European tour for the dissidents—the Borczaks and the four who made it over with them. We can hope that the Dealer will see the tour as an abatement of danger. As far as he's concerned, Borczak can only tell us bits and pieces of the

Bern project. Hopefully, the Dealer will read the tour as proof that we couldn't add up the bits and pieces to the whole of his plan.''

Nick smiled. ''And one of the cities on the tour will be the location of the Dealer's personal diary.''

''Right,'' Hawk nodded.

''What's our cover?'' Tori asked.

''Amalgamated will give the tour top news coverage. You and N3 will go along to do the covering.''

''When is go?'' Nick asked.

''In two days,'' Hawk replied. ''It will last a little more than a week. In the cities that don't interest us, you'll serve as guards and reporters, filing your stories with the greatest emphasis on the connections between the dissidents' claims and the upcoming Bern events. In the city with the diary, you will locate it—and then 'liberate' it.''

''Once we've done that,'' Tori said, ''the Dealer will know the game. What's to keep the Russians from backing out?''

''Timing and pressure,'' Hawk answered. ''At some point late in the tour, the President will be responding to all the press you two have been providing. Publicly, he will offer the dissidents his own personal invitation to attend the conference. Privately, he'll offer the Soviets a chance to discuss parameters in closed session. If they back out on the public announcement, it will read like cowardice. If they back out on the private session, we counter by going public. The Politburo would then most probably hang the Premier by his political neck.''

''They'll be there,'' Nick said.

''What makes you so sure?'' Rackley asked.

''The Dealer won't let it go,'' Nick replied. ''I know him. He'll keep the ball rolling and try to get his records back. He'll come gunning for us, I promise you.''

Hawk let a trace of a smile creep across his face. ''That will be very unfortunate for him, won't it, N3.''

Nick's eyes flickered briefly over to the couch. "Stefan and I both have a small score to settle."

Hawk nodded and glanced at the others. "So, to summarize, our situation is this. The six dissidents will conduct their tour, with N3 and N20 as chaperones. The Dealer's records will be obtained at the proper time, and then collated and transcribed by the Borczaks for presentation to the Russians, and, if necessary, the world. They will then go to Bern. In the meantime, we will be working the mole on this end. We'll try to discover the nature of the Soviet information and whitewash it. Beyond that, we will attempt to turn the mole to our advantage. If that proves impossible—we will neutralize him."

"You mean . . .?" Rackley started, his face suddenly very pale.

"I mean," Hawk said, reaching for a cigar from the humidor on the desk and shredding its wrapper, "exactly what you think I mean, Mr. Rackley. Any further questions?"

The room remained silent.

"Then the briefing is concluded," Hawk said, firing up a match and disappearing in the swirling smoke. "Good luck."

CHAPTER FOUR

Jacek seemed mesmerized by the sound of his own footsteps. It was an uneven tread, heavy, plodding steps that slapped the pavement and echoed off the Georgetown brownstones. And there was a meandering uncertainty in the path he trod, a carelessness he made no effort to hide. But then, there was no reason to. Georgetown at four in the morning held no witnesses, just empty sidewalks and streetlights.

Jacek had meant to get drunk, and he carried his present stupor with gratitude. It had been years since he had allowed himself the luxury of alcohol. After all, spies just don't let themselves lose control. But tonight was an exception. He had endured his day at the office, and he had tried to endure his evening at home. But midnight had come, and gone, and the pain would not let him rest.

So he had gone to a bar to seek solace in drink.

But no amount of vodka could erase the stink, the horrible odor, of betrayal.

He had betrayed the artist, his friend who was now without eyes. He had bartered and traded the trust of

Ganicek, and no matter how many times he had called it duty, it still smelled like betrayal.

And then, in the midst of his drinking, the desire for confession had overwhelmed him. With a shaking hand, on bar stationery, he had written the letter.

Now Jacek halted at the mailbox near the corner of his block. He stared at the drop, his hand toying nervously with the envelope in his pocket.

"Courage," he mumbled. "Courage, Jacek! You gave up your integrity years ago. Did you not at least save your courage?"

Jacek stepped away from the box, his pocket still heavy with its burden, and aimed himself toward his apartment, shaking his head. Confession is not the same when delivered by others. You must face the man, stare into the blinded eyes, study the agony you have written into his face. Only then can confession flow.

But that was not to be. Ganicek had made that quite clear. "No one is allowed to see him," the man had said. "I'm sorry, Jacek. Not even the President would bend on that issue. The dissidents are all leaving for Europe tomorrow, and until then, they are under the strictest security. Perhaps when they return I will be able to arrange a meeting."

That's when the pain started, and it would not stand the waiting. So Jacek searched, calling on favors, digging, as he had so many times, finally obtaining itineraries and accommodation lists. Stefan could now be located and the letter written. But the sending was still too great a task. It would mark the end. The confession would be made, and all that would remain was prison, or flight, or death. These Jacek was not yet strong enough to face.

He climbed the stoop of his apartment, moving through the vestibule and up the three flights to his apartment. His thoughts propelled him cruelly. It was not Stefan who was blind; it was he. All these years of blind service, for what? *To* what? To Russia? No. To the Dealer! And what was changed? What had the world gained from his service? Only death. A Speaker murdered so another could take his place. Ganicek elevated in rank so that Jacek could gain even richer treasures to betray.

Insanity!

Wearily, Jacek entered his apartment and let the door slam closed behind him. He ignored the light switch, preferring the solitude of darkness as he slumped himself down into his chair. "Insanity," he murmured, "total insanity."

"And quite, quite careless as well."

Jacek bolted in his chair, instantly sober. The voice was familiar, cold and hard as a knife. He stared into the dark corner from which it had come, his hands curled into knotted balls on the armrests. For a moment the corner revealed nothing. Then came the grinding sound of venetian blinds opening. The streetlight poured through the slats, slashing across the figure of a man.

But even in the semidarkness, it was the eyes that Jacek riveted on—glittering ovals of blue ice.

Those eyes held Jacek for a moment, and then turned toward the window. "You're drunk," said the Dealer. "It is unbecoming."

Jacek let the tension out in a short snort of laughter. "I suppose it is. Very unprofessional, heh?" Jacek slumped back into his chair. "I'll be truthful. I don't feel very professional. But enough of trivialities. To what do I owe the honor?"

The eyes returned. "You are no doubt aware that your artist friend has defected? That he is in Washington at this moment?"

Another laugh escaped from Jacek's throat. "Certainly, comrade. I've been celebrating that very fact. After all, why not? Was it not I who made you promise to spare him? Was it not I that set him up so you could tear out his eyes? And yet, in spite of me, and in spite of you, he is still free. That demands a celebration, don't you agree?'' Jacek's hand raised in a mock toast. *''Naz-drovya,* comrade. To the men who won't bow down.''

The Dealer's move was rapid and deadly. His body flew from the window, his hands gripping the mole by the lapels. With a strength seemingly impossible from so slender a man, he lifted Jacek, raising the man's face until it was inches from his own.

''I am here to save you, you blithering fool, and I will not be mocked. You drew from me a promise, and I kept it. Blindness may be a handicap—may be an agony to some—but it far exceeds the eternal darkness of death. For you, I made an exception, and now I am paying a price that I cannot afford.''

The Dealer released his grip. Jacek dropped back into the chair, his gaze glued to the figure hulking over him.

''You stink of self-pity,'' he growled. ''You see a man blinded, and you wallow in self-contempt. Betrayal is not the sole domain of espionage agents, my friend. Stefan Borczak did not hesitate to sell your soul.''

''What—what do you mean?''

The Dealer leaned in over Jacek, his hands resting on the arms of the chair. ''I may have blinded the boy, but I also employed him. I put him to work in my office. And when he defected, he took that knowledge with him, knowledge that includes you, comrade. And if you think he has not shared that knowledge with his saviors, then you are an even bigger fool than I thought.''

Jacek stared at the man, an icy chill sweeping over his body. ''You're lying,'' he breathed, but the voice lacked conviction. ''He knows? You let him know that I betrayed him?''

The Dealer reached down to grab Jacek's hand. With very little in the way of gentleness, he hoisted Jacek from the chair and shoved him to the window. Jacek stared out over the street.

''Look there,'' the Dealer pointed. Jacek followed the finger to where it led.

Below was a single figure, huddled in the doorway across the street. The figure stood stock-still, eyes drifting left and right down the street. Now and then there was an occasional twist of the head in the direction of Jacek's window.

"A bit late for tourists, wouldn't you say?"

Jacek studied the man below and then turned to face his tormentor. The lights were, once more, slashing across the Dealer's features, one ribbon cutting across the eyes of blue marble. Jacek battled with his emotions, fighting the instincts of survival, desperately trying to choke out the words that rambled in his brain.

"Maybe it's time," he whispered. "Maybe it's well past the time."

The Dealer's eyes widened and then began burning with a heat so intense, Jacek could almost feel it. Then came the hands. The Dealer pushed out his fists, slamming them into Jacek's chest and driving him back onto the floor.

"You sniveling pig! You would surrender? Is that it? You would walk over to them, turn yourself in, rattle on about the sins you have committed—and then be free! Is that the picture you are seeing?"

A knife suddenly appeared in the Dealer's clenched hand, its tip coming to rest at Jacek's throat.

"Tell me," the Dealer growled. "Are those your intentions? Because if they are, I can save you the trouble."

Jacek's eyes strained to find the tip digging into his flesh. Several breaths of air gasped their way into existence.

"No! Please!" he cried, his voice a timid squeak, pathetic, and resigned. "A thought. Only a thought."

The knife lifted and the Dealer straightened himself. Jacek's hand went to his neck, two fingers coming away with the barest trickle of red. He stared at his own blood, absently noting its texture and hue. Just the sight of it staining his fingertips filled his throat with fear. But the fear gave way to confusion when the Dealer spoke again.

"Would seeing Borczak change your mind?"

Jacek stared, his head nodding involuntarily. "But how?"

The Dealer retreated, the knife disappearing into his coat pocket. "At Bern. It can be arranged so that you will have time with him. Would that please you?"

Jacek's brows furrowed. "But he is not going to Bern. I don't understand. What would he be doing at Bern?"

"Trust me," came the voice. "He will be there. Will you run? Will you allow me to get you out of the country if I promise you a meeting with the artist?"

Jacek's head bobbed up and down. "But how? They are watching."

The Dealer thrust out his hand and tugged the mole to his feet. "They are always watching, my friend. That is what makes beating them such a pleasure. I have made arrangements. Follow me."

Jacek stood hypnotized and confused as the Dealer started off toward the door.

"Come," he said. "There is no time to pack. Anything you need will be provided along the way. I have a car waiting. Come!"

Jacek followed, his hand still massaging at his neck, his burden lightened by the thought of facing his friend. The two slipped through the door, moving quickly down the stairway. At the first landing, the Dealer turned, grabbing Jacek by the arm and steering him toward a back doorway at the end of the hall.

At the door, he cracked it open, his eyes flickering across the alley beyond. Then he nodded and stepped through the door, Jacek following. They both moved down the old, wooden porch. Jacek made a move toward the alley, but the Dealer stopped him with an iron grip on the arm.

When Jacek turned to question him, the Dealer slipped a finger over his lips and gestured toward the front of the house. They moved left, entering a narrow footpath that separated Jacek's apartment from the one next to it. There was only the barest crunch of gravel as they made their way down the narrow lane. About ten feet from where the path would enter the street, the Dealer raised his hand and halted.

From his pocket he drew out a small box with a speaker and two knobs. Silently, he gave the red knob at the top two twists. From the garage came the sound of an engine revving, and Jacek's head turned instinctively as he recognized it. His own car was being started. Suddenly the car shot from the garage. Jacek almost cried out. It was only the firm but cautious slam of the Dealer's elbow that stopped him.

Reality dawned as Jacek watched the car speed off. Behind it came other sounds of engines. Headlights broke out, filling the alley with light as they sped off after the runaway auto. When Jacek turned back, he heard the sounds of footsteps from the front of the apartment. Several men had departed their stations to attack, in force, the stoop that would lead them up to Jacek's apartment.

Still the Dealer waited for the footsteps to fade. And then his head peered out, cautiously scanning the street. Then came the gesture to move. Jacek followed him rapidly onto the pavement. From down the block came the sound of a car engine as an automobile, its headlights dark, purred to a stop before them.

The Dealer yanked open the back door and gestured Jacek into the vehicle.

"Hurry," he ordered. "This man will get you away from your surveillance. Later, he will provide you with your escape route. Do what he says. There will be papers, money, and anything else you may need along the way. Move quickly. I will see you again in Bern."

Jacek barely had time to mutter a "thank you," before he was shoved into the back seat and the door slammed shut behind him. As the car raced off, Jacek stared through the rear window at the Dealer's figure in the shadowed darkness. He gave a brief wave, an inept but sincere gesture, as the car pealed around the corner and disappeared.

For several seconds, the Dealer stared at the space the car had vacated. Around him, figures began to appear out of the darkness. The men who had recently rushed the apartment now reappeared on the stoop, their own eyes following that of the Dealer's. The master spy walked over and addressed one of the suited figures.

"The bodies of the FBI men have been removed?"

One of the men replied in a barely whispered monotone. "Everything has been taken care of, comrade. The bodies have been sanitized, and the men are waiting along the escape route. The target will not escape."

"Excellent," said the Dealer. He tossed the box in his hands up to the man he was speaking to. "Radio ahead. Tell them the setup is in progress. Then get in your own car and follow. I don't want any errors. I want your own confirmation of the termination. You know where to reach me."

The man smiled. Even white teeth appeared in a hollow-cheeked face topped with blonde curls. If possible, the eyes that held the Dealer's were even colder than his own.

"I serve," was all the man said.

"I know," answered the Dealer as another car kicked into life. "Call me." And the Dealer stepped toward the waiting auto.

In another part of Georgetown, another pair of eyes studied the empty streets. Nick stood at his bedroom window, a cigarette in his hand, his mind floating. He stared at nothing in particular, just letting his gaze roam the pavement below. He was barely even conscious of the single automobile that turned the corner and drifted by.

"You were downright jolly at dinner. Maybe we should have left it at that."

The voice came from the candlelit dimness in the room behind him. It belonged to Tori Bacchus.

Nick let his eyes flicker toward the chaise where Tori languished, a brandy snifter in one hand.

She was strikingly beautiful, Nick thought. Her dress was a deep blue, belted around a remarkably tiny waist with a silver sash. The narrowness of her waist emphasized the fullness of her hips and breasts. She looked very female and very sensual, although Nick saw no placid softness in her curves. Rather, there was a flowing firmness that promised strength as well as beauty. Her hair, a glossy brown, hung loosely about her sculpted face.

"Sorry," he said, still letting his eyes fill with the sight of her.

It had been a fun evening. The food had been Hunan Chinese, spicy and hot. They had drunk a gallon of hot tea and talked of past times they had shared.

Nick had indeed been jolly and loose. Tori had been warm and receptive. On leaving the restaurant, no words had been exchanged as to their destination, no "your place or mine." They had simply driven to Nick's apartment.

Inside, he had fixed a brandy. When he had handed it to her, Tori had tugged him close and they had kissed. It wasn't the hello or goodbye kind of kiss they had exchanged in the past. It was the kind of kiss that said, "I want you."

But somehow it hadn't happened. Even with his hands running up the fine, curved arch of her back, and her full breasts burning through his shirt to create a havoc of heat on his chest, it hadn't happened.

On the drive from the restaurant, his mind had already drifted back to the Dealer.

"Nick . . .?"

"Yeah."

"Are you smiling or leering?"

"Neither—looking and loving."

"Bull. Your mind's a million miles from here." As she spoke, Tori sat up, tugging her long legs under her. The dress went with them, exposing a long expanse of soft thigh in dark pantyhose.

Nick's eye caught it, and his smile grew. "You have beautiful thighs."

"I'd like to think the rest of me is all right as well, but that's not really what's on your mind, is it?"

"I guess not."

"The Dealer?" Nick nodded and turned his gaze back to the street. "He's nailed you a time or two, hasn't he?"

Nick nodded. "Yeah, a time or two."

"Does the idea of facing him across a negotiating table bother you?"

"A little. It's not the way we usually go at each other."

"Do you even know what he looks like?"

Nick took a long drag from the cigarette. "I've been face to face with him once. It was dark, and there was a lot going on, but I'll know him when I see him. It's his eyes. They're—well, they're strange. An odd, opaque blue. It's as if you can see right through them into his skull. And when you do, there's nothing there. Once you see those eyes, you never forget them."

"You want to know what I think?" Nick turned to stare at her. "My money says you're praying he'll come after us. You'll be sitting there, eyeball to eyeball, and you won't be able to touch him. And I think that's just eating you up inside."

Nick dropped his cigarette in a nearby ashtray and moved over to the side of the chaise. He reached forward and lightly feathered his fingers through the lush thickness of her hair. "You're bright as well as beautiful."

His hand drifted to the inviting, dark hollow between the swells of her breasts. A fingertip traced the swell of one breast and then flicked the piece of jewelry it found there.

"What's this?"

"A gift from my father, a long time ago. I think of it as a good luck charm."

He leaned forward to inspect it more closely. It was a round jade circle, brightly polished, with a grimacing Oriental face carved into the dark green stone.

"An odd piece."

She nodded. "Supposed to be the Shinto god of good harvest."

Nick chuckled. "Must have been a bad year when they carved this one. You always wear it?"

"Even to bed," Tori said, sliding from the chaise to her feet. "Want to see?"

"Think it's safe?"

"Aren't we alone?"

Nick laughed. "Of course we are. That's not what I meant."

"I know."

They both knew. One agent bedding down another was never a good thing. Getting too close to each other in bed might make you too close in the field.

Closeness means caring. And too much caring might mean carelessness—the number one "don't" on the survival list.

But the aura that now surrounded them had gone too far; the erotic electricity that flowed between them had taken over their minds as well as their bodies.

"I don't care," she whispered.

"Neither do I," Nick replied in a throaty voice.

He raised and stepped slightly back from her. God, he thought again, she was beautiful. Her dark chestnut hair was extremely long and brushed to a glinting glossiness.

She was unusually tall and strikingly sleek, her lush
breasts jutting brazenly and defiantly from her slender
body.

Nick was sure from the fit of the skin-hugging dress that
she wore nothing beneath it except pantyhose. It was
difficult to determine since her breasts didn't have the
slightest suggestion of sag. She looked like a chestnut-
haired, pale-skinned, doe-eyed man-eater, and she fasci-
nated him.

He saw her eyes lift and catch him staring at her.
Something in the pit of his stomach stirred. Something
deep in his body responded violently to the sight of her.
He could not look away. He noticed that her eyebrows
were quite arched and that her nostrils flared sharply. She
held her full red lips slightly parted, and they glistened as
though constantly moist. There was a sparkle to her teeth,
and her eyes were a peculiar shade of violet, curiously
fathomless, and welcoming.

"Bedroom?" she breathed softly.

"Bedroom," Nick growled, and they raced each other
for it.

He fumbled with the buttons on the front of her dress. In
seconds it parted. There was no bra, and her breasts were
as inviting and perfectly round as he had imagined.

She moved against him. Nick felt the closeness of her
body, then the touch of her thighs as she pressed the
softness of her curves tightly against him. Her eyes were
closed and her lips were pursed for his kiss. They were
warm and soft and inviting. They came open as he kissed
her and her tongue slipped into his mouth.

Sudden excitement caught hold of him, burning
through his veins like fire. Tori moaned and dug her
fingernails into his back. Her body trembled and her hips
twisted slowly against his.

At last she tore herself away and looked up at him with
glowing eyes. Her large breasts heaved from her labored
breathing.

"Undress, Nick—hurry!"

His guess was right. She only wore pantyhose beneath the dress. In an instant she was totally naked; a white, candlelit figure standing seductively before him. He stared hungrily at her nude perfection as he tore at his own clothing.

Her breasts were even larger than he had imagined, but perfectly formed. Two firm, ruby-tipped mounds of creamy flesh. The circlets were big and dark, and the hard little nipples were now stiff and erect.

She saw him looking at her and gave a throaty laugh.

"Like what you see?" she asked softly.

"My God," he muttered thickly, "you're lovely."

She had a voluptuous, womanly body with ample hips, a smooth, rounded belly, and beautifully tapered thighs.

Suddenly she was tugging him toward the bed. Then they fell together, locked in a fierce, straining embrace. His hand found one of her breasts, felt it rise and fall beneath his caressing fingers. He cupped the soft, swelling mound, then gently squeezed.

Tori moaned and stirred beneath him. "I like that, Nick," she whispered. "Do anything you want to me—do *everything* to me!"

He took both breasts in his hands and squeezed them together. She stiffened beneath him and purred her pleasure.

"Kiss them!" she implored hoarsely.

It was an order, but kissing was precisely what he had wanted to do. He lowered his face to her straining breasts, felt the soft round globes graze his cheek as he moved his mouth from one to the other, his lips parted, his tongue moistening the warm, pulsing flesh. Then her hands guided him until he found and caressed a hot, upright nipple.

"Oh, God, yes—that's it!" she cried through clenched teeth.

Nick felt her whole body tremble, and then she was

writing beneath him, pulling him down to her, clamping him within the circle of her tightening thighs. A shiver went through him as their bodies touched and seemed to melt together in a shuddering embrace.

His hand and then his fingers found the soft, silken moistness between her thighs. Tori's body became electrified. She whimpered and gasped as her passion reached a peak. Perspiration beaded on her lips, plastered her hair to her head, streamed down her glistening breasts, oiled her slick flesh and gleamed on her writhing thighs. Nick drew back slightly and looked at her with awed fascination. Sightless eyes bulging and rolling, teeth bared in an animal grin, head slung wildly from side to side, she rocked and twisted savagely in a helpless paroxysm of pleasure, a convulsion of delight. As he watched her frenzied contortions and listened to her low, rattling cries, he knew he could wait no longer himself.

In one smooth motion, he slid his body between her dancing legs. With a gasp, Tori reached between them and found him. Smoothly she guided him until Nick was deeply inside her.

His entrance was like turning a switch on in Tori's body. Her hips writhed and her back arched as she thrust to meet him.

"Yes, yes, Nick, all of me—take it all!" she cried, her body twisting beneath his in spasms of delight.

Suddenly a deep groan of release burst from her throat and he felt her body cling and shudder against his in sudden ecstasy.

Just as suddenly, Nick's cry of passion matched hers.

Her long legs locked around him even tighter as the final, convulsive spasms of release took over their bodies at the same time. Nick flooded her belly with his warmth as she writhed her way through a climax that left her limp and drained beneath him.

Jacek nearly fell behind the steering wheel and

slammed the car door shut behind him. He sat a moment, his hands running over his forehead. His brow felt warm and moist, and the breakfast he had just consumed sat uneasily in his stomach. He dropped his hands and shook his head, trying to get his eyes to focus correctly.

"I must never drink like that again," he muttered to himself.

He reached to his right and lifted the road map from the seat. He tilted it toward the window, reading it by the parking lot lights. On it was a carefully traced route left for Jacek by the man who had driven him from the apartment.

"Follow this route," he had said. "You will go to Charleston, West Virginia. Once you arrive, call this number." The man had written it out on the map, and then left.

Jacek traced the route with his fingers, finally coming to rest at the tiny dot that marked his present location. He commanded his eyes to focus. *Winchester,* stated the map. Fifty miles had been traveled, too many more still to go. He tossed the map back onto the seat, an effort that seemed to consume all his strength. With his left hand, he stroked at the spot on his neck that the Dealer had teased with his knifepoint.

It itched and burned and sent throbbing hints of irritation with each breath. Jacek suddenly was wracked with a deep cough that threatened to bring his breakfast back up with a vengeance. He gripped the wheel, waiting out the seizure, willing his body to settle itself. Then, as quickly as the coughing spell had come, it was gone. With a deep sigh, and again vowing eternal sobriety, Jacek fired up the car. With one final shake of the head, he moved out from the parking lot, and back out onto the road. Cranking down the window, he let the cool, Appalachian night air embrace him. For a moment, the mountain air seemed to settle him.

"We go, Jacek," he muttered. "We go to Charleston. We go to Bern."

There was one thing that Jacek could feel much better about. The letter had been mailed. The red and blue mailbox had stared at him from across the parking lot, all the way through breakfast. He had debated the choice, and made it. He was already in flight, what harm could confessions do now? And he would see his friend, be able to face him. How much better if Stefan had time to consider his reactions.

So the letter had been removed from the pocket, and dropped into the box. The act, now done, gave him relief, lifting his spirits as the city lights of Winchester faded behind him. He felt with his foot, and clicked on the brights as the mountain road began twisting before him. Why did his foot weigh a thousand pounds?

He dropped the window some more, giving a quick shiver as the air collided with his sweating brow. He flicked on the radio, scooting the dial past an early farm report, and settling on a country station.

"Enjoy it, Jacek," he said. "You will not be getting Dolly Parton in Moscow."

He settled back into his seat, only dimly aware of the sudden appearance of lights in his rearview mirror. He concentrated on the road, occasionally shaking his head whenever the center line would begin to weave in his vision. He only truly sensed the headlights when they began gaining a rate of speed that hinted at trouble.

Jacek fought the growing sense of dread as his eyes jumped from road to mirror. Could the police be looking for him? Was it possible that someone saw the car he left in? Would the police know which vehicle to stop?

All the questions seemed superfluous as the car behind him came to life. Twin blue beacons flashed on, and a siren split the air. Jacek's heart leaped into his throat and his foot pressed against the accelerator.

No! he thought. *Not now. Not before I've had a chance with Stefan. You cannot take me. You will not!*

Jacek was aware of the screech of his own tires as the

vehicle began twisting through the bends of the mountain road. Behind him were echoing squeals as the police car maintained its distance. It was not gaining, but it was not being lost either. Jacek pressed harder on the pedal, his head shaking violently as the road weaved before him, the cut on his neck throbbing painfully with each heartbeat.

He aimed the car down the center of the road, avoiding the sheer mountain face lifting to his left, and the moonlit darkness of the drop to his right. In spite of his efforts, his eyes would still blur, and there was one horrifying minute of fender meeting guard rail, a sickening whine of metal as Jacek bit into the deep turn.

And then relief. For a moment the road straightened, a long stretch of rising highway that slanted its way up the mountainside. Jacek floored the accelerator, suddenly becoming aware of danger in a different form. From around the bend that marked the end of the stretch came a pair of headlights.

He fought with his vision, inching the car over into the right lane. But the headlights approached him at far too rapid a pace, and no matter how many times he shook his head, one impression would not be stilled. The car that approached was aiming directly at him.

Jacek slammed his hand onto the horn, but the lights wouldn't yield. His eyes grew wide with fright as the oncoming vehicle grew nearer, and nearer, and nearer. At that moment, something within Jacek accepted death.

There was no such choice as stopping; it just didn't exist for him. There were only three real choices: the left, and the hard impact of the mountain face; ahead, and the destruction of collision; or the right, and the looming darkness of the drop.

There was no drama to it, no guard rail to crash out a final chord, no hard screech of braking tires behind, no scream.

There was just an eerie silence as the car left the roadbed.

Jacek's life did not even flash before his clenched and weary eyes.

There was only flight.

And descent.

And then the night was filled with the crushing sound of impact.

Inside the car, there was only the briefest sound of exhaled life, as the steering wheel ground its way through Jacek's chest.

CHAPTER FIVE

AMSTERDAM

There was an almost festive feeling to the city night. Nick and Tori silently shared the lifting sensations, the crisp air rising from the Prinsengracht Canal, the lights glowing over the narrow packed houses with their gabled tops, the distant rise of the Westerker Tower chiming out its eleven o'clock carillon. The two moved quickly, past the pubs, past accordion and belalyka ensembles mingling with the revelry, and past restaurants rich with the odors of fish and pastries.

While Tori stared left, taking in the sights, Nick stared right, searching the ranks of houseboats that lined the canal's edge. Finally he saw the one he was searching for. With a tug on Tori's arm, they crossed the street, hopped the iron rail at the embankment, and stepped their way onto the long deck of the boat.

"Hmm, tasteful," Tori quipped. "Vibrant green with red trim. Do you suppose the inside is this subtle?"

Nick grinned. "I think you're in for a pleasant surprise.

Anatole may not be subtle, but he's entertaining. Brace yourself, my dear, to be swept away in style.''

Nick tapped on the door. His knock was answered by a booming bass voice that rattled the walls. "If you are male, depart! I'm not buying anything. If it is a woman, undress and enter!''

Nick called back, "But what if it's neither?''

The door jerked open to reveal a barrel-chested hulk of a man. "If you are one of those types, come back tomorrow. Let me see how it goes with the women first." A loud roaring laugh ended the comment—that, and the almost complete loss of Nick Carter in the bearlike grip of the man's arms. "Nicholas!" raged the man. "Welcome, you son of a camel humper!''

Tori stared in amazement at the man. He was immense, at least six feet five in his sandaled feet, his limbs thick and sturdy. Any thoughts of subtlety were instantly erased by the skin-tight black pants and the brilliant red shirt— open to the navel, sleeves cut to the shoulder—all to give the coarse flaming red hair that coated his body the room it needed to breathe. Topping the giant body was a freckled face, its fifty-five years of life carved in stone and surrounded by more flaming red tangles of beard. The skull was as bald as a cue ball.

The man released his grip on Nick and grinned into N3's face. The two front teeth were solid gold and gleaming. "I have been expecting you, my dear, dear friend.'' His eyes then darted to Tori, taking her in, leaving no doubt of the appreciation they were receiving from the sight. "My, my, my, my, my,'' he crooned.

Then he moved toward her. From what she had seen of the man's hugs, Tori reacted almost defensively to the approach, cringing backward a few steps. But he stopped short of her, gripped her hand with a touch that was surprisingly gentle, and raised the palm to his lips. Tori let out a small giggle as the beard brushed against her skin.

The giant's eyes twinkled. "It tickles, no?" His free hand dusted through the shaggy facial hair. "It drives the women wild. 'Anatole's bush' they call it. It can tickle you in the most delightful ways, my sweet lovely. And the head!" The hand rose to slap against his pate. "It can do things you have never dreamed. I swear it!"

"Nick. Help!"

Nick stepped over and slapped his friend's broad back. "Anatole, she is overwhelmed by your charm and awed by your beauty. But she has promised her aged and dying father to remain a virgin."

"A virgin!" the giant groaned, and with a deep sigh he lowered Tori's hand. "Ah, well, I must respect the vows made to the ancient and infirm." With a wink he added, "After the funeral, however, visit again—who knows, eh? But enough! Enter, good friend and fair virgin. Bless this humble home with your company!"

Anatole turned and burst back into the boat. Nick and Tori followed. The boat was long and narrow, with two rooms. One was a sitting room with a small kitchenette in the corner, the other, the bedroom.

Tori stood awed at the decor. It was a cluttered museum of knickknacks and junk, from the zebra skin rug on the floor, to the stained glass wall that separated the rooms, to the player piano with its top lifted and ferns billowing out from the interior.

"Your pleasure, Nicholas? The usual?" Anatole bellowed. "And for the lady, the same?"

Nick nodded, and he and Tori settled themselves onto what served as the sofa: a small ship's dinghy with its side cut out and piled high with pillows. Anatole moved to the kitchen counter and swept aside a stack of dirty dishes. He opened one of the overhead cabinet doors, grumbling slightly as two or three empty bottles fell out. Brushing them aside, he gave the cabinet a quick search, and with a cry of triumph, pulled out an ancient dark bottle.

He turned to display it to his guests. "Ambrosia! My own creation. There is nothing like it on this earth." As he dug for two glasses, Tori leaned in to whisper to Nick.

"Do I dare ask what it is that we're about to consume?"

Nick returned the whisper. "I've never quite figured it out. It's a liqueur, Anatole's own recipe, but what it consists of is a secret that neither Anatole nor the human palate will reveal. It's surprisingly tasty, but brace yourself."

Two glasses pounded onto the pillows between them. The cork was torn from the bottle, and a mysterious red-amber liquid filled the glasses. Nick and Tori accepted them as Anatole grabbed a chair and sat to face them.

"To life!" he bellowed, raising the bottle. "Good, bad, or indifferent, it sure beats the hell out of anything else!" With that, he took a giant swig from the bottle.

Tori and Nick gulped at their own drinks, Nick watching delightedly as Tori's eyes grew slightly misty and then her voice croaked out its approval.

"Mmm, smooth," she gasped.

"Ambrosia!" boomed the host.

"True hemlock," Nick murmured as the bottle surged out to refill their glasses, and then returned to fill Anatole's mouth.

The bottle came back down with a brush of the man's hand across his lips. Accompanied by a loud belch, the bottle slammed down onto the carved, medieval chest that served as a coffee table. The resultant contact sent nine pornographic magazines, two African fertility idols, and an agate ashtray rattling to the floor.

"Business now, yes?" Anatole grinned. "Later we can revel!"

He lumbered from his chair, his finger touching his lips to indicate silence. Moving to a corner of the room, he began cranking on an ancient Victrola. From the table by its side he lifted a record. Carefully he blew away the dust and set it on the turntable. There was a moment of loud scratching, a muttered curse, the scream of a needle scraping across plastic, and finally, the sultry, wobbling voice of Edith Piaf.

His mission successful, the giant returned to his chair and leaned toward his guests conspiratorially. "Just a precaution. No one listens to Anatole—not his women, not his friends—so why should the Red bastards? But anyway, it is safer this way, heh?"

He then sent a finger up into the air, a signal to wait. Once more he leaped from his chair, this time to another corner occupied by a huge Louis XIV desk. The desk was piled with papers, papers that began flying back and forth, then up and down, always to the steady muttering of curses. With a final slam the papers landed, half on, and half off, the desk. For a moment the giant stared at the desk in bafflement. Then came apparent inspiration.

A small vase was lifted from the desk, peered into, and greeted with a smile. Then came massive fingers rooting into the narrow opening. Then another loud curse. Then the sound of the vase smashing on wood. A sheet of paper was lifted from the fragments and returned, along with the giant, to the chair and the bottle.

Anatole smoothed out the paper and held it up for examination. "Notes," he winked, as Nick and Tori studied the scrawl across the paper, both trying to decipher the language.

"Italian?" guessed Nick.

"Ancient Latin," corrected Tori.

The giant shook his bald head. "Etruscan!" he beamed. "An ancient Italian civilization. A dead language. Who could read it today? I am not even certain I understand it! But I wrote it, so I can read it, heh?"

Tori gave Nick a very uncertain stare while Nick tried desperately to keep the smile from his face and return the look with assurance. Nick's *having* assurance was not in doubt. Anatole was eccentric, but brilliant, and—when the circumstances demanded—deadly beyond measure. It was *communicating* the assurance that Nick found difficult. Fortunately, Tori seemed to accept it all in stride.

Meanwhile, the giant studied his notes, hummed along with Piaf, and with a final nod wadded up the paper. He popped it into his mouth, and downed it with another swig from the bottle. It took a second for everything to clear his throat, and once it had, the dialogue commenced. With it came a subtle, but noticeable change in the man's expression. Bushy brows knit in concentration and vibrant green eyes grew gray and chilly.

"The message is from *Skylark*."

Nick mentally translated the code name into the real one: David Hawk.

"He says first, the mole has flown. No one-man flight, he says. A real operation."

"When?" Nick said, his own eyes narrowing.

"Just before you left. Maybe four, maybe four-thirty. You had watchdogs, and they did not report. A car was sent. No watchdogs. No mole. Poof!"

Nick quickly analyzed the implications. This was no mole running in panic. Jacek had obviously been given a great deal of assistance in his escape—the kind of assistance the Dealer supplied so well.

Anatole read Nick's thoughts. "Watchdogs are for police and frightened old women. Traitors should not be watched; they should be killed." His barrellike arm mimed a gesture of a knife slicing the human body from groin to throat.

Tori shivered at the obvious violence in the man. Nick spotted her look.

"Anatole served Dutch resistance during the war," he murmured to her. "By the time he was fifteen years old, and the war had ended, he was running half of Amsterdam on his own. He saw a lot of friends get turned in by informers."

"Dogs!" Anatole growled, repeating his gesture as indication of how they were dealt with.

"Since then," Nick said, "Anatole has been working freelance with AXE and is as dependable as they come."

There was a new look in Tori's eyes as she reexamined the massive man sitting across from her. He seemed to sense the mingling of curiosity and admiration in her stare. There was even a hint of a blush on his face before he waved it off again.

"Stop, Nicholas!" he boomed. "My face will heat up, catch fire, and my beard will burn me to death!"

"All right," Nick chuckled, "no more compliments." And then the smile disappeared from his face. "Is there any idea where the mole skipped to?"

"Not at the present," Anatole replied. "Just, poof! But Skylark is searching. The scum will be found. It is assumed the *Ice Man* wants his little pet at home. It is my understanding the vermin would be very helpful to the Russians at Bern."

"It seems to me that the Dealer is covering his bases," Tori offered. "If he can get Jacek to Bern, he can still stage his little charade."

"You're right," Nick nodded. "And that would complicate our plans considerably."

"For once, I make a demand of Skylark," Anatole said, his voice quiet and cold. "It is the Ice Man that is running this, yes?"

Nick nodded.

"Then I go with you. I will be tour guide for the Polish birds. And I will be there when the Ice Man comes. I will be with you when he dies, heh?"

Nick didn't answer immediately. He stared into those eyes, gauging the consequences of the plan. The giant sensed the uncertainty.

"If I do not go with you, then the rest of the message will remain here." A hand slapped against his belly.

"And you can go digging through the canal tomorrow to find it!"

"That's blackmail," Nick chuckled.

"Absolutely!" the big man thundered. "Is it effective?"

There was light laughter from Tori. "I don't know, Nick, he sounds serious. Personally, I'd like to work with him."

The giant opened up in a smile that filled the room with gold reflection. "Trust a virgin, Nicholas. They never tell lies."

Nick smiled and yielded to the combined pressure. "All right, I'll clear it with Skylark. But Tori takes you shopping, and *she* picks the clothing. Agreed?"

"But of course!"

"Now, what else did Skylark send?"

Another finger stabbed into the air, and then another pause as Anatole moved to turn the record over. He returned, and with another sweep of the bottle refilled the glasses.

"A slight change of plans. The Ice Man is suspicious. It will not do to further those suspicions. The tour will follow the first four cities as intended. Publicity will be held to a minimum. Each city will be followed by an invitation to the next. Keep the bastard guessing, heh? You will play up each appearance as scheduled, but the location of the next appearance will not be announced until the previous one has finished.

"Then you will announce cities five and six: city five to be scheduled for the opening day of Bern, city six to be announced at day two of Bern. City six is to be Berlin." Anatole's brow furrowed. "This makes sense to you, heh?"

Nick nodded. Berlin was the city that held the Dealer's diary.

"Good. Anyway, you do not go to city five or city

six,'' the big man continued. "You go to city four, which is Munich, and then you disappear." For a moment Anatole paused, his eyes digging into Nick. "Berlin is important, yes? It is close to Munich, is it not?"

Nick flashed a look that told Anatole not to ask too many questions.

"But what do I know?" The giant shrugged. "Anyway, you go to city four, and then you desert the tour for operation *Retrieval*. Once this has succeeded, you are to go directly to Bern. It is very important that the artist go with you. His role at the conference has grown."

"Is he to be a counter to the mole?"

"Yes," Anatole nodded. "If the Ice Man produces his resource, Skylark wishes to produce his own. You will choose your own sanctuary in Bern. But Skylark made it very clear that day *one* of the conference was critical. You are to move on your own, and you must bring the artist— and the package—with you to Bern. The package must be wrapped and ready to be given then. This is all clear?"

"Crystal," Nick replied. "Now, there are certain things I will need you to do."

A cloud of doubt crossed Anatole's face. "You must clear this with Skylark first. You must not tell me until this is done, correct?"

Nick grinned. "It was cleared days ago, my friend. Would I chase the Ice Man without you to harp and criticize every step of the way?"

"You mean, you intended for me to go all along?" Anatole blinked. "You just wanted to see an old man suffer?"

Nick grinned and nodded.

The giant turned to Tori, his face beaming. "You do well to be with this one. He is good! Almost as good as me!" He leaned close to her, whispering conspiratorially. "But he is lousy with virgins. Avoid him at all costs. Save that for the funeral, and me, heh?" Then he swiveled to

Nick. "Now, what is it you need of me, my friend?"

Nick began to inform Anatole exactly where he fit into the scheme of things.

Once outside the boat, the music continued to drift down the canal in the Amsterdam night. With it came other sounds, specifically the gentle hum of a generator attached to a Volkswagen van. It was parked directly across the canal from Anatole's vibrant green abode.

Inside the van was another sound—the whir of a laser. Its beam was trained carefully on the houseboat window. Its sensitive rays received and recorded the minute reverberations of human speech as sound waves collided with the glass. A computer churned, taking the laser's information and translating it back into speech. Slowly its round, silver type disc cranked the vibrations back into printed word.

There were two men in the rear of the van, technicians. One was an acoustical physicist, a man to whom sound was merely waves and numbers and mathematical constants. The other was a musician, a man gifted with perfect pitch and trained to turn notes into number values.

Together they would take the voice of Edith Piaf and reduce it to its skeletal, scientific basics.

The musician would note an A: 220 Hz logged. A low D: 196 Hz. On and on it would go, until a printout would emerge.

Then the physicist would make adjustments, compute for timbre, for volume, for slurs or shaded notes not quite perfect on the Hertz scale. He would then feed the whole into the microchip miracle of computer electronics. Slowly, Edith Piaf would disappear. Her contribution to the tape would reel within the machine, be reversed, and then erased.

What remained was the random mathematics of human speech—imperfect, inflective, aphonic leaps of sound that rolled out of the typewriter in clear elite typeface—to travel down the length of wire to the headphones at the front of the van.

Two other men sat in the front. The driver wore the headphones, one ear covered to take in the words from the house, one ear bare to take in the words from the man next to him. The second man silently contemplated the events being recorded on sheets of printouts growing before him.

They were heartless men, one blonde, with a face sculpted in granite, the other calm and poised, like a cobra. Both had eyes as cold and emotionless as tombstones.

The man with the papers dropped them on the dashboard, his attention turning to the back of the van. "What do you estimate the transcription delay to be?"

"Minimal, Herr Dealer. A minute, maybe. The record they are playing is *a capella*. Fortunately there is no instrumentation to compute, only the voice. I estimate a minute between reception and final printout."

"Well done," answered the man, his attention returning to the driver. "Piaf," he snorted. "Such a pathetic taste in music."

The driver shrugged. "They live in the past, these war heroes. Spies who still cover conversations with Piaf also still slip potions into drinks!" His smile revealed even teeth, icy white.

"Stone Age heroes," added the Dealer, "in a computer age world. What are they discussing now?"

"The diary. They will make the four city tour, ending in Munich. There will be two more cities on the schedule, but they will be merely cover. The strike on Berlin will be launched from Munich. The Dutchman will accompany—"

The Dealer cut him short, patting at the papers on the dash. "I can read, my friend. It is no more than I expected when I removed their precious Jacek. It is the *details* I need. How, my blonde friend, *how* are they going to strike?"

The man concentrated for a moment on the information pouring into his ear, then turned to the Dealer. "They wish to avoid normal channels. They feel you would be certain to get wind of any attempts in a town you yourself had selected for security reasons."

The Dealer chuckled. "Very wise, indeed. Also, very true. Continue."

"They will contract the job through an independent. At the moment, they are discussing names of possible candidates."

"Candidates we will be sure to make available. Go on."

"Wait—Mercury and the girl appear to be leaving."

All speech halted as the door to the houseboat opened, and three figures made their farewells. The parting was brief, with Nick and Tori stepping off into the Amsterdam night, and the giant returning into his home. From behind the Dealer, the clatter of activity halted. From next to him, the narrative continued.

"They have settled on two possibilities, both Berlin regulars. It has been agreed that the Dutchman will try to make contacts tomorrow. Mercury and the woman will stay with the tour. They will join each other in Paris. The Dutchman is to have the contractor meet them there for interviewing. From there, they will all continue on as per the schedule."

The Dealer laughed hollowly. "No, my friend. Not *all*. The woman is becoming something of an interference. I think it is time she was removed from the scenario. Paris will do nicely. You will arrange it. Nothing that smacks of reprisal, strictly underground all the way. Is that understood?"

The driver removed his earphones and nodded. "Understood."

"Good. Now there are two other matters to be covered. First, contact your man back in Virginia. I think it is time for the mole to be found. By the way, that was very well handled. You are certain it will appear to be accidental?''

"No doubt whatsoever.''

"Excellent. Once you have arranged that, contact the Berlin contractors. Encourage them to be unavailable in the strongest possible terms. Also encourage them to supply *your* name as an alternative. Make it very worth their while, my friend. Make it worth their very lives.''

"You wish for me to handle the strike on the diary?''

The Dealer smiled. "*Naturlich, mein Herr*. It would not do to have them fail, now would it?''

The blonde man returned the Dealer's mirthless smile. "And you, I take it, will be handling the dissidents?''

"Some,'' the Dealer replied, his eyes floating down to his watch. "The first is being taken care of even now, by hands as thorough and competent as mine, I assure you. The poet Janusz is being treated to the time of his life.'' The eyes returned to the driver, the smile chilling. "Quite literally—the very *last* time of his life.''

The poet Janusz sat on the edge of his hotel bed, his body slightly stiff from its efforts, his back tingling with the reminders of long, feminine nails digging into him. She had left an hour before, but the erotic aura of her presence, even her scent, remained in the room to remind him of what had transpired between them.

Janusz's mind and his body sang epics of gratitude.

What a heavenly face she had. And her figure—made for love.

Janusz rose from the bed and, with a slight strut, walked across the room. He wheeled the bathroom door wide and studied himself in the full-length mirror attached to its back.

He was not a man anyone would consider handsome. To grant that he was even "pleasant looking" would be a gift. It was a weathered face of fifty-one years, a body that had never been toned or shapely; he was nondescript to a fault. But he had values. His mind was rich and sensitive and deep.

But he had taken decades of rejection; the mocking of Polish girls, young and old, about his frail body and his gaunt face that looked so much older than its years. Janusz had turned that mockery into verse, transcending a world that was callous and unseeing.

His gaze flickered over his shoulders as he studied the marks on his back. It was proof to him, proof that the whole episode had not been a dream, a fantasy woven from the palette of his imagination. The marks were there, red, welted, just the barest spot or two of broken skin. They tingled, to the point of aching slightly. There was even a slight dizziness, an almost alcoholic euphoria that Janusz attributed to victory—or luck.

He moved back to the bed slowly, fighting the weakness in his knees.

"Too much for you, heh, old man?" he chuckled, easing himself down on the bed. "More than you bargained for—much more!"

But, oh, so wonderful.

It wasn't that he had not intended on companionship. He had heard the reporter and his lady depart. He had watched them take the cab from the hotel front and speed away. He had sensed his opportunity to escape from the protective but watchful eyes of the two agents.

"This is not what I left the Iron Curtain for," he had muttered.

And then he had slipped from his room. Grabbing the street map from the hotel desk, he had wandered the streets that led to the red-light district. There he got the offers; he heard the cries that promised pleasure, but the poet in him would not accept them. He felt sordid, cheap, a traitor to experiences that yielded poems of vast scope and emotion. He wanted elevation, not kicks. He wanted understanding, not sex. So he kept on walking, and finally came back to the confines of the hotel.

From the lobby he had traveled to the bar, to find his pleasures in a glass of wine; one, no more! Alcohol would poison the spirit.

What he found instead, was *her*.

She was beautiful, almost childlike, yet alarmingly sensual. And, wonder of wonders, she sat down next to him. She spoke to him. And she was not a whore. She was a woman unhappy with her life, with her husband, with herself.

Janusz had a second wine, and a third, and finally, the comfort of her arm as he climbed the floors to his room.

And then, heaven. For both of them! Didn't the marks she had made on his back with her nails in the moment of culmination prove it?

A broad smile of happiness creased the poet's weathered fce.

And then suddenly he was struck with an inspiration. He struggled from the bed and on wobbling legs moved to the desk in the corner of the room. There was paper, and a pencil.

He would write. He would take his joy and lay it across the paper in neat, flowing verse. He would even dedicate it! His first poem as a free man, dedicated to the fallen Olek, the poet who had joined him in his flight but had never made it past the Czechs at the border.

But first, the bathroom. The excitement of it all was just slightly too much for him. His back was now aching and his stomach rebelled against the wine, and the activities. He staggered toward the tiny room whose door would suddenly not stand still. He weaved, his knee cracking against the desk chair. His legs were mercilessly heavy. He would vomit, emit the poison, and then he would create—his masterpiece.

There were two more steps, and then there was nothing.

Just an old man, his body spent, his face caressing the carpet.

CHAPTER SIX

PARIS

Nick stood at the arrivals gate at Orly Field. His body was tired, his mind weary, and his spirits sagged. Two days he had remained in Amsterdam, while the tour had traveled on in the capable hands of Tori and Anatole. Nick had remained with the poet, waiting and watching until the life had seeped from Janusz's body. The doctors had made their pronouncement simply. The tubes were pulled out, the machines turned off, and the curtains drawn on the hospital bed.

Such was the end of an old man's life.

"It's idiopathic," one of the doctors had said. "It's viral, with high pathogenic mutation, and extreme iatrogenic complications."

"Say it straight," Nick had demanded.

The doctor had shrugged. "We do not know. It is nothing we have ever seen. The man is from Poland, correct?"

Nick had nodded.

"Then it may be something indigenous to the Eastern bloc nations. If it is localized there, the Soviets would not necessarily share the knowledge with us. They do not boast of their problems, only their solutions."

"Is it contagious?" Nick asked. "Is there any danger to the others?"

The doctor shrugged once more. "There is only one way to find out."

"The hard way, right?"

The nod was sad and resigned. "We will quarantine, of course, at least until—"

But that was where the conversation halted, with Nick making demands, making phone calls, with Hawk and the President lending their subtle power to persuade the Dutch government. In short, a cover-up, with the angered medical team only soothed by the promise of an American research group to aid in studying the virus. The team arrived, and Nick moved on to Paris.

But, while the Dutch government might have accepted events, Nick could not. The potential of disease was not a part of the equation. It muddied the picture and turned the tour into a waiting game. Would anyone else contract it? He would wait and see, and he would keep the knowledge to himself. But he would worry for a while. And worry of any kind was the plague of a mission.

He shook the feelings as the rented car glided to a halt in front of him. He climbed into the seat and returned the affectionate kiss of Tori Bacchus.

"Rough?" she asked.

"Kind of," he answered. "Just an old man whose heart gave out. How have the others taken it?"

"Unhappy, but we've kept them busy enough to keep them from dwelling on it," she replied, maneuvering the car into the traffic flow. Then she grinned. "Wait until you see Anatole. You won't recognize him. He was a brilliant choice, Nick. He's got them all charmed!"

"I trust he's kept his paws off Borczak's wife?"

Her brows knitted slightly. "She's an odd one, Nick. Anatole picked it up right away. *Unmolested*, he called her. 'Watch out for the unmolested wife,' he told me. 'Very passionate, but very desperate.' "

Nick smiled at the impression she made of the bullish Dutchman. "Is he right?"

"Well, I sort of started watching, and yes, I think he's right. Anatole's a three-ring circus, but he does know women."

Images suddenly raced through Nick's mind, of female eyes planted firmly in the carpet all during the briefing in Hawk's office.

"And what does your female intuition tell you?" he asked.

Tori grinned. "An educated guess would be she's jealous."

"What?"

"Really! Think of it. Back in Poland she was the motivator—she got him to stand up and fight. She was his strength."

"And now?"

"It's us. You, and me, and Anatole, and AXE. We control it now. Stefan is the hero, and we're the forces pushing him toward Bern. Borczak and the other men sit on the podiums and tell their stories while she sits in the wings."

"You wouldn't be going feminist on me, would you?"

"It's not a critique, just a fact. I think she's feeling a bit neglected. You've seen how Borczak is throwing himself into it. The man's consumed with getting the Dealer. It's my bet that he's carrying that into the bedroom with him."

"Okay," Nick said. "Supposing you're right, how do we handle it?"

"Well," Tori replied, "maybe just a little more attention. From all of us. Maybe just a bit more effort to include her in the events."

Nick thought for a moment and then snapped his fingers

as an idea hit him. "Why don't you do a story on her? We're supposed to be reporters. Why don't you do a special woman's point of view on Hela. 'The woman behind the man' sort of thing."

Tori's tinkling laughter filled the car. "I've already started it."

"Oh . . . well, I knew it was a brilliant idea," Nick grinned.

"I thought so."

"Any further word from Hawk?"

Tori's smile dropped and business took over. "Indeed there has. We've found the mole."

Nick's head spun in her direction. "Where? How?"

"He's dead, Nick. His car ran off the road, just a few miles west of a little town called Winchester, in Virginia."

"Who found him? Police?"

"No. Some tourist, stopping to relieve himself. He noticed a metallic reflection off the bumper in a stand of trees and phoned it in to State Patrol. Your typical citizen, Nick. He was on an interstate trip and didn't want to get involved—just phoned and ran."

"Then what?"

"The State Patrol investigated, got an I.D., radioed it in, and the computer kicked out the security priority we had placed on Jacek. The Virginia boys promptly washed their hands of it and shipped it over to our investigating team."

"Any luck?"

"For once, yes. The interior of the car was clean, no indication of wherever the hell he thought he was running to. But the trunk was a gold mine. The man had packed two suitcases. One contained clothing and essentials, and one contained a harvest of documents and microfilm."

Nick's eyes narrowed. "Live goods, in a suitcase? Doesn't that strike you as a bit careless?"

Tori shrugged. "Not really. Hawk's guess is that the

information was intended for the show in Bern. Back-up material, or—if we're real lucky—the proof itself, a record of whatever it is the Russians think they're going to throw at us.''

"In a suitcase?" Nick growled.

"Why not? If Borczak hadn't appeared on the scene, who'd have known? The trip to Bern is strictly diplomatic. No customs, no searches, just red carpets and caviar.''

"I hope you're right,'' Nick said, the doubt still obvious in his voice. "How good is the info?''

"Hawk wasn't specific, but it's apparently juicy. So juicy that there's been a slight alteration of plans. Ganicek's been dropped from the delegation. Not publicly, at least not yet, but the change has been made.''

"Why?''

"First of all, if this is what the Soviets are going to come gunning with, it's got Ganicek's name all over it. Jacek bled him dry, Nick. There wasn't anything that passed through that office—Foreign Affairs *or* Intelligence Oversight—nothing that didn't make it onto paper. He'd be crucified, Nick. He'd spend all his time countering accusations and chewing on his own grief. What would that do for negotiations?''

"Not much,'' Nick agreed. "How did he take the news?''

"He roared like a lion. He's been living and breathing this conference for close to a year now. He's not going to surrender easily.''

"But he did surrender.''

"Both Hawk and the President put it out bluntly—tactfully, but bluntly. His entire office is compromised. Borczak can be more effective at the conference, as a *recent* native *and* an Intelligence employee. Also, Ganicek'll be of far more value at home.''

"So who'll take his place?''

"The Vice President!''

"What?'' Nick exclaimed.

"Don't you love it?" Tori smiled, her enthusiasm obvious. "It's the President's own idea. We're going at them tit-for-tat—or better. *They've* lost their mole, but *we've* still got Borczak. *They've* given away their information, but *we'll* still be getting ours. *They're* walking in with the Dealer and the Premier, two exintelligence honchos, so *we* bring in the Vice President, who has had years of experience both in Navy Intelligence and the FBI!"

A long, low whistle escaped from Nick's lips. "So it's head-on-head for real," he breathed. "Should be very interesting. They've occupied opposing desks, and now, opposing offices. There isn't anything the Premier can toss out that the Vice President can't hand back in spades. And when we walk in with the Dealer's records, the Vice President will be able to judge the information from firsthand experience."

"Exactly," Tori nodded, and then noticed the frown on Nick's face. "What's wrong?"

"I don't know for sure," he replied, shaking his head. "It's just a lot to swallow in one sitting. It's also pretty damned lucky, and *that* always makes me a bit nervous. It's a hell of a lot of good fortune just because one son-of-a-bitch falls asleep at the wheel."

"Maybe," Tori shrugged. "Also, he didn't just fall asleep. He was sick. He was running on about two barrels and just slipped off the road."

Alarm bells sounded in Nick's head as he whirled in the seat. "Sick? How? What did he have?"

"No one seems to know. The body was pretty chewed up. But the autopsy revealed some kind of virus. But what it was—no one's saying, or no one knows."

Nick's hand went to his brow. "My God," he muttered.

"What is it—is something wrong, Nick?"

"I don't know," he replied. "I'm not sure—yet." He leaned back in the seat and stared out the window, his brain whirring, trying to fit the pieces of this jigsaw puzzle together.

The car slid to a halt before the Hotel le Colbert, a six-story building of eighteenth-century architecture tucked quietly into one of the narrow alleys of the Left Bank. Together they left the car and entered the lobby.

"Nicholas, you son-of-a-whore-dog!"

"Oh, God," Tori winced, "the Dutch Goliath. Forgive me, Nick, but I think I'll just trot over to the desk and check for messages. You deal with the reunion!"

"Chicken," Nick grinned, and turned to accept the giant arms.

What he got instead was a sight he thought he'd never live to see. Anatole stood, his arms outstretched, his face awaiting the judgment of his friend.

"The virgin, she has some taste, no?" he cried.

Nick stared at the neatly pressed three-piece suit that struggled to contain the body within. The beard had been trimmed, a delicate fringe of tapered hair that gave the Dutchman the air of royalty. Anatole noted the gleam of delight in Nick's face and winked.

"Not to worry," he said, his hand slapping against his chest. "Inside? The same old dog. I promise you."

"Of that, I had no doubts," Nick laughed, clapping his hand on the man's arm. "You look tremendous. I'll warn you right now. There's not a woman in Paris who will be able to resist you."

The giant waved off the thought. "Ach! Women? Paris, Amsterdam, Timbuktu—they are all the same! Take off the tailoring and roll down the bed, and there is still only one thing that will bring the smile to their faces, heh? *That,* my friend, has not been tailored!"

"I heard that," laughed an approaching Tori.

Anatole leaned into Nick. "For a virgin, she has big ears!" he chuckled. "But come, my friend. We have company in the bar. The man from Berlin. You wish to meet him now?"

Nick perked at the news. "Yes. Right now."

Tori cut in. "Nick, before you do that, look at this!" She handed him an envelope. "Anatole and I thought it best if any mail came, it come through us first."

Nick stared at the envelope. It was addressed to Stefan Borczak; the return address was a small neighborhood bar in Georgetown—the Granada. The name was familiar. It was a tavern only three or four blocks from Nick's house.

"Look at the postmark!" Tori pointed.

The faintly smeared blue marking was difficult to read, but clear enough. *Winchester, Virginia*.

"Jacek," he breathed.

"Who else?" Tori said from beside him. "Should we hand it over or check it out ourselves?"

Nick debated for a moment, giving honest consideration to the concept of runaways from communism who suddenly find their mail being opened and checked. It could have some unpleasant repercussions. Nick decided to compromise. He handed the letter back to Tori.

"Stefan is blind and Hela may not understand the subtle aspects of English. Why don't you give them a hand and read it to them. Then we'll all know what it says."

"But it could be anything, Nick. Jacek was a mole. It could be lies. It could be damaging. It could explode."

"I know," he nodded, thrusting the letter further into her hand. "And it could also give us the key we're looking for."

Tori shrugged and took it at last.

Nick watched her move toward the elevator. There was something in her walk, the tilt of her head, the slant of her shoulders.

Was she going to take the letter to Stefan or not?

He was about to call out to her when Anatole's booming voice broke into his thoughts.

"We go, heh? The man is waiting. And, Nick . . .?"

"Yeah?"

"Listen to this man. Feel him. He comes highly recommended, but there is something—I don't know what it is. He seems more like the man we seek than the man himself. You judge—tell me if an old man is imagining things, heh?''

Nick patted the massive shoulder. ''I'll judge him carefully. Trust me.''

Anatole nodded and they headed for the bar.

Beyond the high arch was a long room with a bar running along one side. The ceiling was high, with open oak beams darkened from years of smoke layering them.

They paused a few seconds to let their eyes adjust to the dimness, and then Anatole gestured to a table in a far corner.

Nick nodded, and a moment later they were seated across from the man they would interview.

To the layman he would rate little more than a glance. But to Nick the man looked what he was—a killer. It was in the easy, slouched body, internally tense, externally at ease. It was in the unwavering slate gray eyes that stared back at Nick from a hard, chiseled face.

In fact, the only lightness about the man was his mane of blonde hair. It almost shimmered, even in the bar's dim light.

He smiled. His teeth were perfect, even, and gleaming white.

For some reason the smile brought a sense of distaste to the forefront of Nick's mind.

He pushed it away. Personal distaste was not a factor of judgment in cases such as this. The underworld was peopled by the outcasts, the sadists, and the insecure. You got used to dealing with them, even if they did offend one's sensibilities.

Nick nodded his greeting as Anatole opened the events.

''The man I spoke of,'' he said, gesturing toward Nick. ''You will call him Alpha. That is all you need to know of him. Alpha, this is Herr Schwartz.''

Nick noted the alias with a smile. Schwartz was German for *black*. In espionage terms, the equivalent of *Mr. Smith*. In the future, if the interview proved productive, the Herr Schwartz would be dropped and forgotten. The blonde man would simply be *Omega*.

"Credentials?" clipped Nick.

"A reputation," the blonde replied icily. "And a history."

Nick waited, but nothing else was forthcoming. His eyes narrowed. "I have fifty thousand marks to play with, Herr Schwartz," he said evenly. "If you are willing, I might choose to play with you. But I don't know your reputation, and I am too busy to read histories. We can play games, if you like. We can play chess or we can play monopoly. The choice is yours."

The killer's stare remained leveled on Nick, then he shrugged. "Sixteen contracts, seven assassinations, five kidnappings, four espionage. All successful, all very high priced."

"Jail?" Nick growled.

"Never," came the answer. "And, to save us both time. Morals: none. Involvements: none. Limitations: few, if any. Training: the streets, mercenary service, and the terrorist underground. Any other questions?"

"Price?" Nick said.

"Seventy-five thousand marks directly payable to a Swiss account."

"Dependability?"

"Infallible," came the reply.

Nick looked over to Anatole. His answer was merely a shrug that hinted at "your choice." Nick returned his concentration to the blonde killer.

"Are you familiar with a man called the Dealer?" he asked.

For the briefest of moments, the eyes seemed to waver and the granite features broke ever so slightly. But the voice when it came was ice cold and even.

"I have heard the name. I appreciate the skills involved. The man is a genius."

Nick waited. "And?"

"It would be quite a challenge."

"Are you equal to that challenge?" Nick asked, carefully reading the response.

The blonde man leaned forward, his hands resting on the tabletop, his fingers toying with the wineglass before him. The glass suddenly shattered into fragments, wine dribbling onto the table—all from the force of the man's grasp. And then he turned his hands, palms up, on the table.

Both Nick and Anatole stared at the palms. They were coated in red, but at no point was the coloration due to anything but the Burgundy wine the glass had contained.

Shattered crystal, and not even a nick of torn flesh.

"Does that answer your question?" the blonde said, a slow smile creasing his features.

Nick looked from the tabletop to the slate gray eyes staring back at him. "Seventy-five thousand marks will suit you?"

The smile broadened. "Plus expenses. The Dealer is a very special—problem. Research will have to be carefully done. Execution, the state of the art. You agree?"

Nick resented the arrogance, the confidence, and the leverage. But he had seen the fulcrum. The man was stone, an iron automaton of death and effectiveness. But, in that one moment when the Dealer had first been mentioned, the man had let the human parts take charge. He had hesitated. That showed respect, and that implied caution. The man could do the job, and Nick felt the price a small hurdle to overcome.

"How much?"

"A hundred thousand."

"Is this a final figure or will there be adjustments in the future?"

"A hundred thousand, Alpha. Period. Even though you will see that I am well worth twice that. Do we have a bargain?"

Nick's answer was succinct and more than face-saving. The tumbler before him lifted and shattered, the remaining Scotch joining the Burgundy on the table. His palm lifted, presented itself, and then arched its way toward the blonde man's side of the table.

"We have a bargain," Nick said.

The man took the outstretched hand firmly in his grasp, a grin of reluctant admiration displaying his white, even teeth.

"We have much work to do," Nick growled.

The blonde nodded. "Give me the general plan you have in mind."

"Briefly the situation is this. It's a hit-and-run operation. The Dealer is the goat. We move quickly, and then we're gone. You can work out the details with my red-bearded friend here. In the meantime, we need you to set it up. We'll appear the day of the strike, and we'll disappear right after. Any qualms?"

"None," came the reply.

"Then excuse me," Nick said, rising from the table. The man did not bother to rise himself, nor did Nick expect him to. "You will have four days."

"It's a shame you can't stay longer," the blonde grinned. "Berlin is beautiful this time of year."

"Maybe the next time," Nick replied. "Until later, *auf Wiedersehen*, Omega."

CHAPTER SEVEN

PARIS

Nick stepped out from the elevator and onto the carpet runner that ran along the third-floor hallway. He felt satisfied with the Omega interview. For the moment, he allowed the lift in his spirits to erase any thought of disease and death.

He moved down the hall, eyeing the room numbers, coming at last to the door marked three twenty-two. He paused a moment, preparing his opening line. A smile crept over his face as the idea came, and his hand rose to twist at the metal knob of the doorbell.

Then he froze.

From within came a sound, a rough sound, a gasping of human effort. For one second Nick considered the possibility that Tori had company, but the thought fled as quickly as it came. Again the sound, a hoarse rasping, almost a cry.

His hand flew into his coat, withdrawing Wilhelmina, even as his body two-stepped its way backward in the hall.

Then he reversed and launched his body at the door, his foot slamming at the woodwork. There was a groan as the aged lockwork fought to hold, and the door cracked into streamers of raw lumber. A second kick, quickly delivered, destroyed what little resistance remained. The door flew open, small fragments of wood and iron scattering onto the suite's carpet.

Nick followed the door, his back slamming against it, Wilhelmina trained on the small cubicle of the bathroom. It appeared empty, at least from what was visible to Nick.

He dropped to his haunches and swept Wilhelmina in an arc, pointing her down the narrow hall. The sitting room also appeared empty. Nick moved. He ran down the hall, leaping as he neared the opening into the room. He flew, hitting the carpet and rolling back up to his haunches.

His eyes fell on a second doorway, the one that led to the bedroom. A dark figure in a leather flight jacket was moving toward the opening, his hand reaching to slam the door. Even as he steadied Wilhelmina on the target, Nick's mind was clicking off a description: North African, Arabic; Moroccan, by all appearances.

Not that it mattered all that much. Nick was prepared to squeeze the trigger on any form that was not Tori's. The finger tensed even as the door began to close. But suddenly there was a movement from beside him. The huge wing chair to his right gave a quick jerk up, and the back crashed down on him just at the instant the gun exploded.

His shot drifted to the left, chewing a hole in the door itself, but leaving the black jacket behind it clean of any damage. Nick rolled with the chair, letting it settle over him, curling his legs up and twisting his back onto the floor. He counted two quick beats, and then shot his legs out.

The chair flew up into space. From over the top, Nick could make out another dark Moroccan face. Then the chair slammed into the man's chest. From the side of it appeared the gleaming blade of a knife. The man took the impact, grunting, and then, with the sweep of his hand, he shoved the chair aside. His other hand came up ready to toss its pointed missile, but the battle was rigged from the start. You just don't try to outrace a Luger.

Wilhelmina barked only once, and the Moroccan's chest exploded into a red blossom. He sailed backward with the impact, pounding into the room's corner, his back sliding down the wall. Nick rolled, leaped to his feet, and took the bedroom door with only one violent slam of his foot.

Again the black-jacketed figure was visible, this time half in, half out of the open bedroom window. Behind him, already safe on the balcony, was another man. Behind him, his body shimmying down the balcony rail ironwork, was a third. Nick took aim again, his sights settling on the man about to drop from the balcony's view. He fired, but again the shot ran far from course.

This time it was not furniture that threw him off; it was the impact of a well-trained foot on the underside of his outstretched arms. It came from his right.

Jesus, another one? Nick thought. It's a damn army!

This one had plastered himself against the wall, his sole function to give his compatriots time to depart.

The foot landed solidly, driving Nick's arms up into the air and jarring Wilhelmina from his grasp. Nick could hear the gun as it careened off the wall and thudded onto the carpet.

But what consumed the majority of his attention was the second blow from the man's foot. With lightning speed the foot withdrew from its first contact, recoiled, and flew back out to catch Nick in the ribs. The blow drove Nick into the door. It was only the quick, athletic spin of his torso that saved him from breaking his shoulder on the doorjamb. Instead, he twisted and took the shock over the breadth of his back, neutralizing the impact.

Nick's eyes flew up to evaluate his situation. The man was huge for a North African. Not tall, but incredibly wide and sturdy. There was no gun and no knife, just the hard gleam of the eyes and the stiff curl of a sneer that said this man was confident and capable with just his hands. The man moved toward Nick, his scarred face a living record of just how many others had fallen beneath his skills.

Nick sidestepped, faked a kick to the man's groin, and arched his arm out and up. The hard edge of his hand chopped with brutal force across the man's throat. The head lolled and the eyes glazed as the pupils rolled up into his skull.

But somehow he stayed upright and came on again, his huge arms flailing.

Nick was ready.

He bent swiftly and came back up under one of the loglike swinging arms. In the same movement he brought his knee up. This time it was no fake. Bone met genitals with crunching force.

There was a gurgled scream of pain and the man slumped against Nick. He steadied the gasping form, took aim, and repeated the chopping blow to the man's neck.

This time he connected perfectly with the windpipe. Slowly the man's knees bent and he fell, facedown. Bending quickly, Nick retrieved Wilhelmina and raced to the window.

A quick sweep with his eyes gave him the picture. Number one was on the balcony to his left. Two was careening down the fire escape to join three, who was already in the alley.

Nick's appearance at the window drew two quick shots from number one on the balcony.

Their plan was obvious. The one on the balcony would hold Nick off until his two buddies found cover in the alley. Then they would do the same for him.

Nick moved to the corpse. Sliding his left arm under the man's coat clear to the neck, he hoisted the body up in front of him. Without a second's hesitation, Nick charged the window, using the body as a ram and a shield.

Gunfire shattered the air the instant they appeared. Nick could feel the slugs from the side and below pound into his shield. When he felt the windowsill strike his thighs, he heaved the body through and rolled behind it. He hit on his side, rolled, and came up firing.

Wilhelmina's first slug caught the guy to his left dead center in the chest. The second slug tore away part of his face, but it made no difference. He was already dead and falling in a perfect spiral to the alley below.

A slug whined near Nick's ear and raised hell with the bricks behind him. A second hit the steel grating near his feet and careened off into the air.

Nick moved like synchronized lightning down the fire escape. For half a floor he slid on his heels and butt. For another he rolled. To further spoil their aim, he crossed up his movements by actually taking a whole section of the iron stairs in one bound.

Twice Nick returned their fire during his descent. He wasn't sure, but he thought he had nailed one of them in the leg. This was confirmed when he hit the cement of the alley and rolled to his knee.

One was helping the other who had a limp leg dragging behind him. Both had had enough and were fleeing the scene as fast as they could.

When the one with good legs saw Nick raise Wilhelmina, his comradeship disappeared. He dropped his buddy and took off. Nick sighted on the man's left thigh and squeezed off a shot. Just as he fired, the man's feet hit something slick on the alley concrete.

Nick's slug hit him on the way down—dead center in the base of his spine. Nick knew the man was dead before he hit the ground.

At least one is left alive, Nick thought, racing to the groaning figure across the alley.

To Nick's surprise, the man had more life left than he had thought.

Nick had barely reached him when his good leg came up in a well-timed kick. A stiletto-toed boot connected perfectly with Nick's wrist, sending Wilhelmina flying from his hand. At the same time, the man got a hold on one of Nick's ankles and twisted.

The man was wounded, but he was still quick. Nick's back had barely touched the concrete when the man was over him. A dagger glinted in his hand.

Easy, Nick thought, watching the arm arch too high before its downward swing. Nothing to it.

True to his thought, Nick caught the man's wrist in his own left fist without any trouble. He was about to put him to sleep with his right, when the alley exploded.

The result of the explosion was a very large hole in the man's chest. Nick rolled him away and came to his own feet, his head jerking toward the direction of the explosion.

Twenty feet away stood the tall blonde, a Walther still smoking in his hand, an enigmatic, toothy smile on his face.

Bastard, Nick thought. Stupid bastard!

Nick stared at the body kicking out its last breath at his feet, then turned and moved down the alley. His eyes were flaming as he approached the blonde killer. The man was coolly slipping out the clip of his Walther, holding it up and counting the shells that remained.

Nick's hand gripped Omega at the wrist, clamping down with viselike pressure, jerking the arm down and twisting the man's face into his own.

"Why?" he spat. "He might have talked."

"It was your life or his," the tall blonde shrugged. "He had the dagger."

"Bullshit," Nick hissed back at him. "Not good enough. I had him all but disarmed, and you know it."

Omega wrenched his wrist from Nick's grip. He spoke as he pocketed the Walther.

"Two years, that's why. Two years of mercenary work in the Spanish Sahara. Two years of watching *Polisarios* butchered by Moroccan scum. Any other questions, Alpha?"

"One hell of a time to settle old scores," Nick hissed, then spotted Anatole's red-bearded face emerging from the rear of the hotel.

"Goddamn!" the man cried, seeing the carnage in the alley.

The words were barely out of his mouth before the nearby streets were filled with the monotonous tones of French police cars.

It was time to move and move fast.

Nick slid past the blonde and stepped directly in front of Anatole.

"Get rid of him," Nick growled, choking down the anger within him. "I don't want to see his face again until Berlin. Set him up and ship him out fast."

"Will do," Anatole said, motioning to the blonde, who was already moving down the alley in the opposite direction from the sirens.

Nick took the fire escape stairs five at a time, a gnawing fear in his gut at what he would find back in Tori's room.

From the bed he followed a thin trail of blood into the bathroom. She was in the tub, which explained why he hadn't seen her when he had first quick-checked the room.

Her dress had been partially ripped away. One breast gleamed nakedly. Just at the top of the breast's swell was a single stab wound. From the size of it, the wound had probably been made by a stiletto. It was small, neat, and there had been very little bleeding—which meant she had died quickly.

Thank God for that, Nick thought, if for nothing else.

Her hands were still tied, clenched over her abdomen. From one clenched palm Nick spotted two ribbons of a broken gold chain.

Nick pried open the fingers and tugged the remnants of the gold chain from them. He had expected the jade amulet to be still connected to the chain and held in Tori's clenched fist.

It wasn't.

He lightly swung the chain between his own thumb and forefinger. Slowly a stab of pain hit him in the gut, and regret contorted his features.

It happened—often. It always did and always would. Death came with the territory. But Nick's guts boiled at the reality that it had come to Tori.

His eyes drifted from the lifeless form in the tub to the chain and back again.

Words drifted up from his memory. "My father gave it to me a long time ago. I think of it as my good luck charm. I wear it all the time."

Suddenly his heavy brows furrowed and lines of intent concentration seamed his forehead. Again he stared down at the silent, white face, now wondering at the priorities of the dying. Why had Tori taken the amulet off just before she was killed? And why such a final death grip on the remnants of the broken chain? Had she been in such a rush to remove it that she hadn't even taken time to unfasten the clasp?

Immediately Nick bolted through the rooms of the suite. He ripped her purse and suitcases apart. Then he began going after the obvious hiding places that would be overlooked by most.

Nothing.

Then he went through the places where something would just be idly thrown, as if it belonged there.

He found it in a drawer, tossed into a pile of lacy

underthings. With bated breath, he opened the carved teak lid.

The amulet was inside, and directly beneath it was Jacek's letter with the Winchester, Virginia, postmark.

He left the amulet but retrieved the letter. Turning it over in his hand, he studied it carefully, noting the back flap. The letter had been opened. Flashes of the lobby encounter between Tori and himself ran through his mind.

She had defied him. She had obviously gone right from the lobby to her room, ripped open the letter and read it. Then, before she could reseal it and go to Borczak and Hela, she had been killed.

If she had meant to take it to the Polish couple at all.

She hadn't. She knew she only had moments, so she hid it and then kept the broken chain in her hand to tell Nick, to clue him in that the letter was important and that it was still in the suite.

He was about to withdraw the stained piece of paper from the envelope, when loud voices from the alley interrupted him.

Police. Soon they would figure out that the carnage had all started in the very room where he now stood.

Quickly he glanced over all of Tori's things. Like a good spy, there was nothing to acknowledge her as an agent. This done, he slipped into the hall and took the stairs to his own floor three at a time.

All the time, the letter burning a hole in his palm.

CHAPTER EIGHT

Since it was off-season, the big Boeing 747 was barely a third booked when it lifted off the runway at Orly Field. After a sharp bank, the plane turned west and began to climb through the clouds. In minutes it reached its cruising altitude and leveled off to head for England and Heathrow Airport.

Nick lit a cigarette and let the smoke burn deeply into his lungs before exhaling it. Several seats in front of him, in the No Smoking section, he could see the back of Stefan Borczak's head, and the perfect coif of his wife in the adjoining seat. Directly across the aisle sat the other two dissidents, one nodding and the other deeply absorbed in a newspaper.

The seat beside Nick was empty. He'd arranged it that way before boarding. He needed privacy, time to think. No puzzle, if it was worth attacking in the first place, had a quick or an easy solution. But this one had more pieces that didn't fit than anything Nick had ever seen before.

And Jacek's letter didn't help.

With a very audible sigh, he reached into his inside coat pocket to retrieve the letter for another read.

"Is something the matter, *monsieur*?"

Nick looked up. A very tall, very blonde flight attendant stood in the aisle by his seat. Her face held the usual look of professional concern behind the equally professional smile.

"Nothing that can't be solved by a drink," Nick grinned, arresting the movement of his hand.

"A cocktail?"

"Yes—uh, no. A Campari, please, with one cube."

"Oui, monsieur."

As she moved away, Nick studied the rhythmic movement of her well-shaped derriere and the gliding walk of those long legs. Tori had been tall, with legs that made the rest of her body move like that.

Cursing under his breath, he finished tugging the envelope from his pocket. The sheet of paper inside was water-stained in several places, and one corner looked as though it had been constantly worried by nervous fingers as the writer composed.

My dear friend Stefan,

Call this letter what you will—a confession, an apology, a written reenactment of my sins—but know that it had to be written.

I betrayed you. From the beginning so very many years before, I betrayed you. Long before I even knew you, before the night of our flight in Berlin, I was groomed for what was to come. My defection to the West was only a ruse to put me in a position to spy for the KGB and the Dealer. I have become what is called a mole.

My life these last years I considered my duty. I was troubled by what had happened to you, but I was able to remain content and do the job I was trained to do.

Until you defected and I was forced to kill. I am not a strong man, this I admit. I am a clerk, nothing more, trained to use my eyes and ears and cyphers to report what I see and hear. They never told me I would have to kill; yet they forced me to do it.

Even as I planted their vile instrument of death, I began
to have doubts. My rise in rank, allowing a greater amount
of service to Russia and the Dealer, was no longer an
excuse.

I can go no further with this deception. I have planned to
turn myself in. Because of this, I will probably be prevented
from ever seeing you, even as they prevent me now.

I don't ask for your forgiveness, dear Stefan, for the pain
my betrayal has caused you. The Dealer promised that you
would be spared that night. I foolishly trusted him. Yes,
you were spared your life, but you were denied your freedom, and your sight was taken from you.

For that I blame myself and ask that you understand.

Jacek

The main message of the letter was written in a reeling
scrawl, as if the author were sleeping, or drunk, or doped.
There was a postscript beneath the signature written in a
far steadier, more precise hand.

Have seen the Dealer and he has explained. He has told
me that you have been informed of my duties in his grand
scheme. I do not blame you, my friend, for informing on
me. Thankfully, all I have said above can now be explained
in detail. The Dealer has agreed to get me out of the
country. Believe it or not, my friend, but we will meet again
after all. I will see you in Bern. Until then . . .

But he had never made it to Bern, Nick mused. He
hadn't even made it out of the country. And if he *had* made
it, what did Jacek plan to do with his suitcase full of
incriminating material?

If, indeed, the suitcase had been his.

"Your drink, *monsieur*."

"What? Oh yes. Thank you."

She set the drink on the tray in front of Nick and then
moved aside to let someone pass. It was Parshev, the
younger of the two male dissidents.

Parshev nodded slightly to Nick as he passed and made his way to the rear of the plane and the restroom. Nick sipped his drink and returned his gaze to the letter.

Besides the main text and the postscript, there were penciled notations in the margins. Nick had seen enough of Tori's small, printed hand to know that they were hers.

It was the dead woman's notations that made the letter so much of a puzzle.

Each reference to "kill" was underlined. "Rise in rank" was circled, and beside it Tori had written in "to where" and "with who." Over "Berlin" she had jotted Nick's Killmaster designation, N3, and a question mark. Several lines encircled "planted the instrument," and beside it, in pencil, "What? Bomb? Gun? How kill? Check with Nick! Check with Hawk!"

On the back of the page, Tori had penciled in several questions. Evidently her mind had been flying after digesting the letter, and these were her notes probably meant to be gone over later with him. "Who Jacek kill? Speaker? Why?" "Ganicek to Speaker? Could be answer to rise in rank—maybe!" "First part, Jacek going to turn self in. Sees Dealer, runs. Why? Just to see Borczak in Bern?" "If Dealer in Wash. to see Jacek, where Dealer now?" "How did Jacek know Borczak to Bern? Postmark is prior to final decision on day and place. Also prior to news release!"

It was obvious to Nick that the Dealer had told Jacek that Stefan would be in Bern. And while it wasn't obvious, Nick figured that the Dealer had urged Jacek to run, and then had him killed.

But Jacek hadn't a mark on him beyond the bruises from the accident. Or did he? The body showed traces of illness, a virus. . . .

A movement coming up the aisle caught Nick's attention. It was Hela. Quickly he double-folded the letter and slipped it into the side pocket of his jacket.

"May I sit here for a moment, Mr. Carter?"

"Sure," Nick nodded. "And after all the days together, I think we can make it Nick . . . Hela."

"Thank you."

Nick eyed the woman as she slid gracefully into the seat beside him. The dress was a dull, in-between brown, snug around the hips, but cinched at the waist so that the top bloused, almost becoming baggy.

Her face sported little makeup, just some lip gloss and a little blush on the cheeks. The eyes were bare, in their natural state, and now they darted from the front of the plane, to Nick, to her lap.

The eyes, when they met Nick's, were almost cold. They seemed to look but not see. They had glanced at Nick, but not really acknowledged his existence.

Nick's gut reaction now, as it had been several times before when he had been this close to Hela Borczak, was that the slim figure beneath the clothes was constructed of pure ice.

Or maybe she was just that way toward him. No, Anatole had felt something akin to Nick's feeling about the woman.

"Could I have a cigarette, please?"

"I didn't think you smoked."

"I don't, only on occasion. It—it makes me calm."

Nick was pretty sure this woman was always calm. Nevertheless, he extended his case and then lit the cigarette she withdrew from it.

"My, they are strong, aren't they?"

"Don't inhale," Nick shrugged.

Silence.

"I'm sorry Tori couldn't accompany us to London. I miss her."

Nick merely nodded. The AXE boys in Paris had done a good job of keeping Tori's name out of the press. She was merely a female victim. Nick had explained to Borczak, Hela and the two others that she would be joining them later.

"I will be glad when it is over—all this." She punctuated her words with a cloud of uninhaled smoke.

"We both will. Or I should say, we *all* will."

"Perhaps Stefan will return to me then."

Nick didn't reply. He remembered Tori's words about Stefan's obsession with the Dealer encroaching on the bedroom. Again he glanced at Hela. Again he could almost feel her coldness. Maybe he didn't know women after all, but it seemed to him that Hela could care less if Stefan left her alone.

As if to defy Nick's thoughts, her hand crept up to cover his where it rested on the armrest between them.

"I feel as if my only purpose in life is to be the seeing eye dog for a fanatic bent on revenge."

Her words were emphasized by a squeeze of her hand. Almost imperceptibly, her voice had dropped a full octave into a throaty whisper.

"A very lonely seeing eye dog, at that," she added.

Jesus, she can shift like a forest fire being fanned by a strong wind, Nick thought. But far beneath the smoldering look that had entered her eyes, he could still detect the marblelike coldness.

He was just about to search for an adequate reply, as well as a subtle way of extricating his hand, when it was provided for him.

From several seats in front there came a stifled scream, followed by a rasping, gagging cough.

Nick looked up just in time to see Mazelik, the fourth male dissident, stagger into the aisle clutching his throat with both hands. The man's face was a glaring, bright red, and only the whites could be seen in his rolling eyes.

"My God, what's wrong with him!" Hela cried.

Nick didn't take time to answer. He placed a hand on each seat back, tucked his legs, and vaulted over Hela into the aisle.

In seconds he was past the rest of the gasping, frightened passengers and had Mazelik in his arms. The man could get no air, and each anguished wheeze sounded like his last.

Nick swiftly whirled him around and stretched him out as gently as possible in the aisle. It took all the force he could muster in both hands to force the jaw open. Once it was done, Nick checked the tongue.

Mazelik hadn't swallowed it yet. To make sure he didn't, Nick started to reach for his pen. Wrapped in his handkerchief, it would make a substitute tongue depressor.

"Here!"

Nick looked up. It was the long-legged stewardess, and in her hand she held the real thing.

"Good girl."

Nick applied it sideways inside Mazelik's mouth and then ripped the man's shirt open. The wheezing had progressed now to what sounded like a death rattle. Nick balled his hands in a single, clublike fist and began to apply strong but even pressure on Mazelik's chest in the vicinity of the heart.

Up! Down! Up! Down! Up! Down!

Rest! Rest!

Up! Down!

Fetid air filled Nick's nostrils as Mazelik exhaled but didn't take in a new breath.

Nick stopped the movement and dropped his ear to the man's chest. A second later he rolled back to his haunches.

"Is he—" the stewardess asked.

"He sure as hell is," Nick growled between gritted teeth. And then he remembered. "Parshev—shit!"

Nick lurched to his feet. With flailing arms, he thrust curious passengers from his path. Like a frustrated and angry bull, he surged toward ths rear of the plane.

Once there, he swept his eyes over the doors of the four lavatories. Only one was occupied.

"Parshev!" he cried, pounding both fists on the door.

There was no answer.

Nick had expected none.

Leaning against the bulkhead behind him and using the handles on the other two lavatory doors, Nick lifted his legs into the air. His feet shot forward, and the soles of his shoes made a sickening, crunching sound as the door's lock shattered on impact.

The door only opened a few inches. But it was far enough to see the dissident's body, with his head sprawled in the sink.

Nick pushed the door open a few inches more, far enough to get his own head inside.

"Jesus Christ," he whispered under his breath. "The poor bastard didn't even have time to pull his pants up."

Nick's hands half-covered his eyes as they stared at the embossed nameplate on the desk before him: DAVIDSON HARCOURT-WITTE. Idly, Nick wondered if Davidson Harcourt-Witte was Cambridge or Oxford. For sure he had been Eton. Eton was almost as much a prerequisite for MI-5 as Cambridge or Oxford, in the upper echelons, that is.

Beyond the plaque, its owner sat red-faced and fuming.

"Good God, Carter, did you have to radio Heathrow and slap a quarantine status on the *whole plane*?"

"There were two bodies—"

He was ignored. "And you'll have to settle it with the Froggies about taking command of a French airliner."

"I showed them proper authority," Nick replied, trying to keep the boredom out of his voice. Harcourt-Witte's anxiety about British etiquette and French bureaucracy was making it hard for him to concentrate on important things.

The man was still raving about irate quarantined passengers and sputtering French pilots when an aide came in, deposited a report on the desk, and scurried out. The aide had barely hit the door when Nick speared the document.

"Son-of-a-bitch, Carter, have you no manners?"

"None," Nick replied, pacing as he speed read.

"Autopsy report: two males; descriptions; manner of death: heart attack, but traces of virus found in blood; special report; computer correlation; virus aligns with that found in Bulgarian defector; gave dates; also same virus detected in two Czech defectors killed in London. . . ." Nick let out a low whistle. "Damn!"

The expletive sent Harcourt-Witte back in his chair. His voice, when he spoke this time, was far meeker. "What?"

"Washington routinely ordered a blood analysis of our dissident, Janusz, who died in Amsterdam, run through your files. Why wasn't this picked up before?" Nick slapped the report down on the desk and pointed to the meaningful paragraphs.

"Ah, yes, the umbrella killings." Nick groaned. "I really don't know, old boy. These things do take time, you know."

"Almost as much time as it takes a mole in MI-5 to be discovered."

"See here now—"

"Get up!"

He did, and Nick took his place behind the desk. "Is this a safe line?"

"Yes."

Nick reached for it and then stopped, smiling up at the other man innocently. "May I?

"Well, I suppose. It is a business call, isn't it?"

"Jesus," Nick growled and placed the call to Dupont Circle.

A lot of things made sense now. For instance, Nick was pretty sure what the "instrument of death" in Jacek's letter meant now. And other things, already spotted by

Tori, also became clear.

"Hawk here."

"N3, London."

"Go ahead. You're being taped."

Nick brought his superior up-to-date on the letter and the latest fatalities.

"Can you redo the autopsy on Jacek and shoot some blood samples here to MI-5 for clarification?"

"Shouldn't be a problem," came the reply.

"And I don't think the stroke suffered by the Speaker of the House was, in fact, a stroke."

"How so?"

"In his letter, the mole mentioned a raise in rank. With the Speaker dead, Ganicek was next in line to not only the office, but also the tremendous information available to that office. That would mean that, if Ganicek had the information, our mole, Jacek, would have access to it. I think that's what he meant about 'raise in rank.' "

"If this is all true," Hawk said, "how do you want me to prove it?"

"Exhume the Speaker's body."

The thunder from the other end of the line was deafening, ending with a growled, "You are nuts. No way—the family would never agree."

"Okay, okay," Nick moaned. "Can you get access to the Speaker's personal effects on or about the time of his death? Such as personal things from his desk—both at home and in his office. Any personal things from his clothing drawers."

"In other words, everything the guy owned?" Hawk said, exasperation in his voice.

"You've got it," Nick replied. "At least everything that touched his body. And especially anything that could have punctured his skin. If you find anything like that, have it analyzed immediately and send that analysis post-haste, along with everything else, to MI-5."

"I think you have some idea already of what we'll find."

"Maybe," Nick replied. "Maybe some kind of a heart arrester that Western doctors don't know about yet."

"That all?"

"That's all. How soon?"

"Very soon."

They rang off and Nick sat back in the thick cushioned chair with a sigh. He knew now that the virus was no plague, or anything that approached it. The plague was the Dealth Dealer himself. He had been following the team of dissidents himself, or through a henchman, and systematically had been killing them off one at a time.

But why one at a time? Why not all at once?

And then it clicked.

"If you don't have a plague, the next best thing is to create the *impression* of one!"

"Plague, old boy?" muttered Harcourt-Witte. "What on earth are you talking about?"

"Get your boys off their asses," Nick said, bolting for the door, "and you'll know when I do."

CHAPTER NINE

Nick tapped on the door and waited. It was opened a crack, and then pulled wide.

"Stefan isn't here."

"I know," Nick replied. "He's in the hotel bar having an after-dinner drink with Anatole."

Hela nodded, and then a little light seemed to go on in her eyes. It brought a smile to her lightly rouged lips. "Then you dropped by to see me."

"That's right," Nick said, letting his eyes cover all of her beneath partially hooded lids.

As it had on the plane, much of her cold demeanor dropped away with the smile. Not all, but most. More than ever before, she had an air of femininity about her. Nick wondered if it was the robe. It was an azure, silky affair that clung like a sheath to her tall, model's body. Contrary to the dresses she usually wore, the robe fit snugly. It flowed over her breasts, separating and accenting them.

"You're very lovely this evening, Mrs. Borczak."

The smile grew. "Is that a compliment or a Nick Carter statement of fact?"

"A little of both."

"If this is a social call, I think—"

"It isn't," Nick said, stepping by her into the suite. "But I'll have a drink while we play twenty questions. I ask, you answer."

Out of the corner of his eye Nick watched the smile fade from Hela's lips and the coldness return to her eyes. He also noticed the slits on each side of the robe when she shrugged and turned to close the door. They went all the way up to the softly rounded undercurves of her buttocks.

"What'll it be? as you say in America."

"Scotch, neat."

As she built the drinks and walked back to where Nick had perched on the arm of a sofa, he got another shot of adrenaline from what his mind called her new or different look.

The simple sash on the robe was drawn tightly about her tiny waist. It did marvelous things to the ample curves of her hips and breasts. She slid the drink into Nick's hand and then lowered herself into a lounging position on the sofa nearby. She landed with one leg drawn up, so the robe split open, the bottom falling away. Nick's eyes had no trouble following a large expanse of creamy thigh up to the barest suggestion of jet black pubic curls.

"Is that an invitation?" he asked, sipping the Scotch.

"Is that one of the twenty questions?"

"Touché" he said. "No."

"Then it's a comfortable way of sitting."

As she spoke, she held her drink in front of her eyes, studying him over the rim of the glass. It was meant to add mystery and sultriness to her look. Like the lounging pose, it was too studied. Nick wondered if it was natural or learned.

He guessed the latter.

"Do you love your husband, Mrs. Borczak?"

For the barest of seconds her eyes clouded, the knuckles grew slightly whiter around the glass, and the arched leg made a slight movement to close and cross over its mate.

"Why do you ask?"

"I ask, remember? You answer."

"We are not lovers, if that's what you mean. No longer, at least. We are more like companions now."

"But you are married?"

Her head swiveled to him. Now the eyes were like chunks of jade ice. The lips were sealed, a thin red slash above a firm, defiant chin. To Nick's surprise, her reply, when she spoke at last, was truthful.

"No, we're not married. At least not in the usual sense. We exchanged vows between ourselves and I took Stefan's name. It's a common thing in the Eastern bloc countries where the church doesn't reign supreme.

"Did the vows you exchanged between yourselves include a vow of fidelity?" The look never wavered, but the lips returned to their state of closed silence. "Okay, another one. When did you exchange these vows with Stefan?"

"Six years ago this month." Not a blink, not a quiver, or a second's hesitation.

"What day?"

"The eighteenth."

"Where?"

"Warsaw."

"Was Stefan blind then?"

"Of course. Where . . .?"

Nick verbally bolted on, trying not to give her time to think, even though he knew she didn't need to. "What was your maiden name?"

"Obstrawski."

"You were born in East Berlin."

"I was born in Cracow."

"What section?"

"The Bakslackvia section, in the south."

"Ever been to the U.S. before?"

"No."

"Your English is perfect, even the slang."

"I received a very good education."

"Where? Russia?"

Only a slight pause before she said, "Partially."

Now Nick paused, sipping the Scotch and letting it burn all the way down before speaking again. "When were you recruited to do your training at the Verkhonoye House of Love in Russia?"

Goddamn, Nick thought, she is good. The eyes continued their cold appraisal, and the lips even managed to twist into a rather wicked grin.

"How did you find out?"

It was Nick's turn to smile. "I didn't. It was an educated guess. There are times, when viewed by another agent, that your training sticks out like a ringer in a pickup game."

"Ringer?"

"An American expression you should know."

Hela put both hands on the glass and finally dropped her gaze from Nick's eyes. She stared into the amber liquid for several moments before speaking. When she did speak, there was just the suggestion—just the *right* suggestion—of a quiver in her voice.

"You know about Verkhonoye? What goes on there? The training they give young girls to become sparrows?"

"Yes," Nick replied, trying to take in every part of her at once. He didn't want to miss a single clue, and it was impossible to know from where it would come.

"I was thirteen and a virgin. I was orphaned and put in a State home when I was ten. I had talent as a pianist. I thought it was that talent I was going to explore when I was picked to go to Moscow."

Nick glanced at Hela's fingers. They were long, tapering fingers, thin but with obvious strength. But it was the nails that riveted his eyes. They too were long, and manicured to almost sharpened points. There was a slight sheen to their surface from a clear polish.

"Do you play now?" he asked idly.

"Rarely, if ever." Without glancing at Nick, Hela sipped her drink and then continued. "At first, when the Dealer put Stefan and me together, I felt like an animal, a piece of meat to be fattened and used. But then Stefan and I grew fond of each other. I saw the core of hate that was consuming him and decided to rebel against my training and the Dealer's edicts."

"So instead of playing watchdog for the Dealer over one of his drones, you become the drone's conscience?"

"Not entirely. I wanted out myself. Through Stefan I saw a way. Is it your turn to pour?"

She held the empty glass up. Over it, Nick could see the sadness in her eyes. But he could also see the icy depths that wouldn't go away.

Hela was either pouring her guts out, he thought, or she was the greatest actress since Sarah Bernhardt.

He took the glass and moved to the bar.

"Stefan and I agreed that if you learned about my KGB background, slight as it was, I would never be allowed to defect with him. Also, it would be impossible for your side to accept the aid that Stefan wanted to give you in destroying the Dealer."

Nick stood directly over her as he placed the drink in her hand. He could smell her perfume, the musky scent of her body warmth, all of her. He could look down the openly draped top of the robe and see the gentle swell of her parted breasts. A tightening sensation gripped his belly and loins.

Tori had been openly sensual. This woman was classically erotic.

Taking the drink, she motioned with her eyes to the place beside her on the sofa. Nick sat and, sensing her start to move close to him, spoke again.

"Who is the Dealer?"

She shrugged. "A man. That's all I can tell you—all

anyone can tell you about him, except perhaps his superiors. And probably very few of them know much about him.''

Nick swirled the liquid in his glass, his eyes darting from it to her, and back again. "I don't know his face," he murmured. "I only saw him once—on a dark night in Berlin, beside a wall. But I saw his eyes, and those I'll never forget. I'll know him by those eyes, but it would help if I had some kind of description beyond that."

"I never saw him."

"What? But that's impossible!"

She shook her head. "It isn't. The only people he worked with who knew definitively that the man they were talking with was the Dealer were blind men."

"You mean you've never seen his face?" Nick asked incredulously.

"Never."

Nick heaved himself to his feet and crossed to the window. Through the London fog he could see people moving along the streets of Mayfair. Was the Dealer down there now, looking up at him, waiting for him?

He could be.

The man was a godamn phantom.

Nick spoke without turning. "Aren't you and Stefan worried about this virus, this plague that seems to be running amok through defectors?"

"Of course we're worried. I'm petrified."

"You should be. You're the only two left."

"There's something in your voice," she said. "Why don't you put it into words?"

Nick turned. She had crossed the room and stood so close now that her breasts nearly brushed his chest. Her scent was stronger than ever, and the dark depths of her eyes were almost hypnotic.

"I don't think it's a disease at all," Nick said slowly. "I think it's a unique kind of poison that acts as a heart arrester. I think a virus is introduced into the bloodstream along with the poison that acts on the respiratory system. And I think the Dealer, or those who work for him, are the ones doing the introducing.''

''Then we're next?''

''Perhaps. Perhaps not. Maybe the Dealer wants to keep the two of you alive—or just one of you. I don't know. Perhaps the Dealer wants to give the impression of a plague, and the further impression that all or most of you contracted it before leaving the Eastern side.''

''But why? What can be his purpose?''

Nick shrugged. ''I'm not sure.''

''You don't trust me, do you?'' Hela said, moving closer now so that the soft pillows of her braless breasts beneath the robe began to spread on his chest.

''Should I? You were originally placed at Stefan's side by the Dealer. The man, like all the rest of them over there, plans long range. You could still be in his pocket, waiting to be used when the time came.''

''I could, but I'm not.''

''But there's no way to prove it, is there?''

The pink tip of her tongue slid forward to lightly run over her lower lip. She had a wide, full mouth, Nick thought, the kind you see a lot in beauty pageants. Her lower lip, glistening now with saliva, was sensuously full. It was a kissable mouth, but Nick didn't forget that it could bite as well as kiss.

''I think, Hela, it would be wise if you went on to Berlin with me, while Stefan goes to Munich with Anatole and the others.''

''You think I'm the Dealer's instrument of death? You think that when the time is right, I'm going to kill Stefan?''

''I don't know what to think. But for insurance, I'd feel better if Anatole had only Stefan to worry about now. Will you go?''

Her eyes bored into his. He could almost feel the thoughts churning as she weighed his proposal.

"I'll go," she said. "Gladly."

"Oh?"

She nodded. "Yes. Because while I'm alone with you in Berlin, I'll prove to you that you have nothing to fear from me."

Her body relaxed, melted against his. She was provoking him, pasting her thighs to his and twisting her hips. He tried to extricate himself, but she held him by the waist and drew him in closer. Her breasts were spread across his chest now, and their heat suffused his whole body.

Her mouth was like a magnet drawing his. He kissed her, their lips barely touching before her tongue was delving deeply inside his mouth.

The kiss was long and deep. It was perfectly executed, everything Nick thought it would be. Just before he lifted his head, he felt those long, perfectly manicured nails tickling the skin and the short hairs on the back of his neck.

"We needn't wait for Berlin," she murmured, her voice low and husky. "I can slip up to your suite as soon as Stefan is asleep. . . ."

He was tempted, for several reasons, as he looked down at her. Her eyes were closed, her breasts heaving. Her lips were parted, soft, her tongue darting between them. She moaned as she brought her body back against his with a jolt.

"Say yes."

"No. Berlin—maybe."

He left her like that, standing by the window. By the time he got to his own suite, there was sweat on the palms of his hands.

He wasn't sure whether it was brought on by desire or a tinge of fear.

The red light gleamed on his bedside phone.

"Carter, five-thirteen. My light is on."

"Yes, Mr. Carter, you have two messages. One was just, 'Call home.' There was no number."

"I have it," he replied. "And the other?" She gave him the number Nick recognized as Harcourt-Witte's private line. "Would you dial that for me, please?"

"Certainly."

Seconds later the MI-5 man's clipped accent echoed in Nick's ear.

"You chaps are fast. Thanks to computers, ours are too. A printout of everything you wanted will be on my desk in twenty minutes."

"I'll be there in ten," Nick said quickly, and rang off.

Nick sat at Harcourt-Witte's desk. The reams of computer printout were spread out before him. It was just after ten and Nick had been poring over them for the better part of three hours.

They were like a book with a few key chapters missing, but they did paint an overall picture.

"More coffee?"

Nick looked up. Harcourt-Witte stood in the diffused glow from the desk lamp holding a teapot. "Yeah, thanks." He poured. "Isn't that a teapot?"

Harcourt-Witte nodded. "I had them make some coffee though. Figured tea, even ours, wouldn't be strong enough for you."

Nick smiled. "You've been a big help. Sorry I was so sticky the other day."

"Pay no mind. You chaps just don't go as much by the book as we do. Suppose it's the frontier thing—independence, cowboys, Indians, gangsters—all that sort of thing."

Nick grinned and saluted the Englishman with his cup as one of the desk's many phones set up a clamor.

"Your call from Washington," Harcourt-Witte said, handing Nick the receiver and moving soundlessly from the room.

"Carter here."

Hawk's voice mumbled and then began to growl.

"Your hunch about the Speaker was right—same virus."

"I know," Nick said, lighting a cigarette. "I've got the printouts in front of me. What about the other?"

"Had a hell of a time getting the family's permission, but we were finally able to exhume the body."

"And?"

"A tiny puncture in the thumb. It was so minute they missed it before."

"In the thumb?" Nick said, and coughed from just one too many drags on one too many cigarettes. "Chances are it was self-administered then."

"That's what we figured." Hawk paused and Nick bit his lip to keep from urging the man on. "We finally found your 'instrument of death' in the things from his office desk. It was a lighter—common brand, made in Japan."

"Shit," Nick said, "hardest damn thing in the world to trace."

"Right, and probably doctored after purchase anyway—which would make tracing it of no consequence. But we were in luck."

Nick's body tensed, his ears came alive, and his nostrils flared like an animal who has just caught the scent. "Yeah?"

"An aide in the Speaker's office remembered that the lighter had been a gift."

"From whom?"

"The aide couldn't remember, but a secretary did remember that it was delivered by Jacek."

"And Jacek worked in Ganicek's office," Nick whispered.

Both men were silent, the static of the long distance line the only sound between them. But Nick was sure his superior's mind was traveling down the same avenues as his own.

Ganicek's political career had a meteoric rise. It was always heavily funded, and his constituency was heavily Slavic, mostly Polish Americans. He was looked upon as an American-born freedom fighter for the rights of those in the old country. He had spent a great deal of time in Poland after the war, trying to stop the Russian takeover of the country of his heritage.

But had that been his real reason for his extended stay in Poland?

"It's a little mind-boggling, isn't it?"

"It is," Nick replied. "I assume—difficult and awkward as it must be—you've started surveillance on the new Speaker?"

"Minute by minute, around the clock. I've also sent top priority, ultrasecret inquiries to Vienna. They'll be relayed on to Budapest, Prague, and, needless to say, Warsaw. Should have a complete reevaluation of Ganicek's background and activities within twenty-four hours."

"I'll need it immediately in Berlin," Nick said.

"You'll have it."

Nick's mind, weary as it had become, was trigger fast now. Ganicek was a popular man. He was to have been the U.S. voice in Bern. Now his duties as Speaker precluded his appearance there. The Vice President would take his place, in a figurehead position. This wouldn't hurt the negotiations that much, because Stefan Borczak would speak of Poland and East Berlin with an even more recent and authoritative voice.

"And, Nick—" Hawk said, his voice breaking into Nick's thoughts like a sharp knife, "—there's something else."

"On Ganicek?"

"No, on the Dealer. We've unearthed a file, an old one. It went through several times, but I spotted it by accident because of this virus and plague business."

"Read it to me; it's worth the time."

Nick went through half a pack of cigarettes, a lot of coughing, and a lot of teeth clenching for the next thirty minutes as he listened to Hawk's gravelly voice read through the file.

At last he finished and Nick could feel the sweat running like a river down the center of his back.

"I'll need a complete copy of that, down to your own notes, by the time I get to Berlin."

"You'll have it. And, N3 . . ."

"Yeah?"

"Cut down on your smoking, or switch to cigars. Those cigarettes will kill you."

"I know," Nick growled. "But at least it takes time to go that way. Our dissident friends weren't so lucky."

Nick let himself into the suite and didn't bother with the light in the sitting room as he moved through the dimness into the bedroom.

He was one step from the door when he sensed something; breathing, a slight rustle of movement from the direction of the bed, a barely perceptible sound that told him he wasn't alone.

Instinctively he reached for Wilhelmina and then thought better of it. There had been enough hell raised with gunplay in Paris. There was no sense doing a repeat of that in London and being forced into yet another cover-up

Quietly he slipped his shoes off and tensed the muscle in his right forearm. Hugo, his pencil-thin stiletto, slid into Nick's palm from its chamois sheath. He crouched and duck-walked over the threshold, and then, holding his own breath, listened for someone else's.

It came, steady and even, from the bed.

He tensed the muscles in his thighs, steadied himself with his left hand on the carpet, flipped Hugo to prepare for a downward thrust, and rolled to his toes for the lunge.

"Nick, is that you?"

The voice came from the bed just as diffused light from the bedside lamp spread through the room. Nick was halfway over the end of the bed, with Hugo raised to strike. He barely managed to stop his forward motion and the downward sweep of the needlelike blade, when he recognized the voice's owner and the bed's occupant.

Hela gasped and her eyes grew wide as she watched the stiletto come down in an arc to stop inches from her bare left breast.

"Waiting in a dark room is a very good way to get yourself killed, lady."

"I—I'm sorry. I started to doze and the light was in my eyes—"

"Why weren't you dozing in your own suite?"

"I wanted to tell you that I spoke of everything to Stefan. He thinks that I should do anything to allay your fears. He has agreed that I should accompany you to Berlin."

"You could have told me that in the morning," Nick said, rolling off the bed to his feet.

"I know."

At the shock of seeing Hugo coming at her, Hela had pulled the sheet up to her neck. Now Nick watched her long, tapered fingers with the long, curved nails slowly roll it down. It seemed an eternity until the sheet was around her ankles, but the view was worth the wait.

Before, in the partially revealing robe, she had been tantalizing. Now, completely naked, she was awe-inspiring. Her off-white body seemed to flower upward from the stark white sheet, urged to expansion and growth by the fire her nudity had awakened in his eyes. Her breasts rose heavy and full from her body. The arch of her hips and the swelling of her thighs was clean and perfect.

"Yes, I could have told you in the morning. That could have waited. But this wouldn't wait until Berlin."

Nick knew women were attracted to him, but he also knew that he was far from irresistible. He was about to tell her to wiggle her way back to her own suite and Stefan, when she stretched out her arms. Her fingers curled back and forth toward him in an inviting motion. The clear polish on the long nails reflected the light, becoming little beacons drawing him forward.

All part of the job, he thought, unbuttoning his shirt—and not entirely unpleasant!

By the time he joined her, he too was nude. Then they met, flesh to naked flesh in the bed. Her thighs and breasts came against him in a practiced, grinding movement. Indeed, every move she made, every nip of her teeth, scrape of her nails, was designed to raise his passion level another five degrees.

He hurt her with his teeth, his hands and his lips. And then he took her, doing all he could to hurt her there, too. But she only squealed in delight and matched his thrusting rhythms.

Time held no sway over their movements. They seemed to go on forever. And then, at his ear, her gasps grew heavy and her lips formed one word, "Now!"

She arched upward, grinding herself against his thrusting maleness. Nick felt her nails dig into his back deeply and then rake upward as she howled out her culmination.

Nick disregarded the pain in his back from her biting nails as he locked himself against her and joined her in fulfillment.

Slowly, with only occasional spasms, they settled down, side by side, into the mattress.

The tumult of passion had barely subsided when Hela opened her eyes and let the mask of desire fade from her face.

"It wasn't—right, was it?"

"It was release," Nick replied, sotto voce. "Sometimes that's all it's meant to be."

"It's hard not to—well, not to be a professional in one's mind, even when one's body is screaming otherwise."

"I know. We're in the same business, remember?"

"*Were*—in the same business," she replied. "It will be better in Berlin, I promise you."

"I'm sure it will," Nick murmured, moving his hand to her breast and closing his eyes.

CHAPTER TEN

BERLIN

Nick dropped a Deutsche mark in the waiter's hand and waved him away. Lightly he ran his hand down the glass of Riesling and then closed his fist around it.

He and Hela Borczak had arrived in Berlin early that morning on a Lufthansa flight from Heathrow. They had checked into a small pension just off the Bahnhofstrasse. A big, flashy continental hotel would be a detriment for the short time they would be using it. Also, it would be easier for Nick, and the local AXE man he had assigned, to keep an eye on Hela's movements and whereabouts.

True to his word, Hawk had delivered. The research on Ganicek and the file that he had read to Nick from Washington had been on the embassy cypher machine at three o'clock that afternoon. Nick had gone through it with a fine-tooth comb and then, with a bound copy of the file in hand, he had returned to the pension.

The tall, blonde killer Nick had coded as Omega had made his contact at exactly six.

"The plan is go. The envelope has been planted at the drop. The ad has been placed in the personals of the *Berliner Zeitung*."

Now Nick sat, and waited.

His hand left the Riesling and he settled back, easing himself as much as possible into the uncomfortable chair. For the moment he was content with his surroundings and the vigil he had kept for two hours. And for the first time since the whole show had begun, he was also somewhat content with the way the scenario was unrolling.

He slitted his eyes, letting the tenseness ease from his body as he collated the last three days' accumulated information.

The letter had been the beginning, the letter he was certain, down in the deepest part of his guts, that the Dealer knew nothing about. Then, of course, there were Tori's penciled comments.

Nick toasted her memory with the Riesling.

Then came MI-5. It had taken a little arm bending, but it had paid off. When pushed, the English service would use the brilliant minds at their disposal.

Nick had been pleasantly surprised that one of those brilliant minds had been Harcourt-Witte when the occasion had arisen. Nick had been sparked by his idle mention of the London murders, murders that were officially described as either heart attacks or death by reason of unknown virus. When Hawk had sent the material from Washington, Harcourt-Witte had jumped right on it.

Then it had all clicked when the London medicos had said, "Right-o, chaps, same disease."

Disease? No way! It was calculated assassination by the master himself: the Death Dealer.

But the real clincher had been the little known file unearthed by Hawk in AXE's own files.

It was a thin file, the record of an AXE disaster. That was probably why it wasn't red-flagged by some minor clerk in the first place. No agency wants to point out its glaring failures, even to itself.

But it was a file with assassination as its result. Because of that, the bureau's computers had kicked it out. And, bless his devious mind and keen eye, Hawk had picked it up.

It was tagged yellow instead of red, meaning "Reference Only." Its conclusion was, *opponent uncertain*. On the identification strip there were several names—mostly aliases and cyphers.

One of them was the Dealer.

It had been a Turkish caper involving two defectors who had come over to the Western side. Both had gone through debrief with flying colors and were considered safe.

One wasn't. He was a plant and an assassin, though it was only surmised, never proved.

In any event, two NATO engineering brains had died of an odd virus, and AXE, as their watchdogs, ended up with egg on its face.

There was no way to exhume the bodies of the two scientists, but Nick was pretty sure that if they could, they would discover that their "virus" matched all too perfectly the deaths Nick had just gone through with his own dissident group—a "virus" that appeared to be indigenous to people important to the West.

The real downer was the second defector. He had come up with the same virus a month after the scientists had succumbed.

The other defector, who supposedly had the key to Soviet ground plans to invade Turkey in the case of war, disappeared.

Nick would bet his life that the defector who had disappeared, leaving so many *infected* bodies behind, was the Dealer.

A movement across the street jarred his concentration.

The eyes came open, wide, as his chair rocked forward. The shop had a customer.

Nick sipped the Riesling and watched—and waited. An exchange, but not the right one.

Nick sighed and lightly flicked his eyes down both ends of the street. The surroundings were not much to boast about. It was a nondescript section of Berlin, not the type of atmosphere the tourists sought. It was a decrepit section, packed with crumbling building fronts and colorless inhabitants. Even the bar in which he sat was sad. A few tables of rotted wood, a bar with stools so packed together, one had to elbow one's way to a seat, and long benches flanking the wall, one or two occupied by drunks too stupefied to depart.

But it had a view, through a clouded, grease-streaked window, that let Nick look out from his perch and study the street.

Again his glance bypassed the squalor to settle on one particular shop. It was a neighborhood shop, designed to suit the local needs: some dry goods, simple clothing, small appliances, and, for the right price, some pleasure from the buxom lady who ran it.

But none of that interested Nick. What did interest him was the wall behind the counter, the wall visible from his vantage point—the wall that contained the ancient wooden letter drops.

For two hours he had watched those boxes, the first hour with hope, the second with certainty. From the time of his arrival, he had remained at his table, drinking his watered wine, paying for the privilege with large tips that guaranteed his sole occupancy.

Across the street the customer departed, and Nick settled back once again to watch.

Again the eyes slitted in thought, musings.

The President and his cabinet were solidly anti-Soviet, as was Ganicek. All of them were high on Bern. The timing was ripe. Elevate Ganicek and you elevate the mole that has been planted in his office.

At least that was what it looked like. The mole—Jacek—was only a tool to be used for a solitary purpose when the time came. Once that time came, he would die mysteriously, taking all the onus of guilt off someone else.

Nick now knew—or had a pretty good guess—who that someone else was.

About the time everything is ready to come down, the mole loses his guts. He's killed, but planted with him is information very detrimental to the Soviet cause.

Planted by the Dealer? Probably. But why?

Because the Dealer is out to screw up both sides. It fits his style. He wants the power behind the throne for himself. It's the Russian way.

Let AXE get the information from Jacek's suitcase, plus the diaries, and the Russian leaders are compromised at Bern.

But how does he compromise the Russian side and still emerge as the *power behind the throne*?

Nick smiled to himself.

By neutralizing the Americans and having the proper club over their Russian counterparts to control them.

The Dealer was a ruthless killer by trade and by design. He was a man who would compromise valuable assets, information or people to gain his ultimate goal.

He learned under a master, the chief of the KGB. And now his master was the Premier of Russia. What if he could master his master and bring the Americans to their knees at the same time?

Ultimate power.

Power through fear, manipulation, and assassination.

The United States comes to the conference all readied up to do verbal battle. A head-to-head meeting is scheduled for the first day, very neatly arranged in closed session. and what happens? Accusations are slung and counterslung, and sins are compared, and violations weighed, and understandings are reached, and agreements are made whereby both parties decide to mutually drop the whole thing and get on with the conference like gentlemen and scholars.

Where did assassination fit?

Nick chuckled to himself, but it was a mirthless sound. The whole scheme was too huge, too all-encompassingly galling and evil, to have any humor in it.

After weighing everything he had learned, Nick had come to one conclusion. The Dealer was an assassin by trade. All of his coups in the past had been based on assassination. It was the fulcrum from which all of his upward mobility, his power and his reputation had pivoted since he had first emerged so many years ago.

The research on Ganicek, easy to get when you knew what to look for, had given the key to the rest of the scheme.

Ganicek, a bright young man, had been born in the United States, but had been taken to Poland by his socialist father as a small child. Years later, he had welcomed his younger brother to Warsaw from America—his younger brother who had come to Poland to fight communism. But instead of finding a way to fight communism, the younger Ganicek had found a grave, while the older Ganicek had returned to America in his place.

In America, the elder Ganicek worked hard in two capacities. One, to gain political prestige and power. The second, to bide his time until his real purpose—the purpose of his master, the Dealer—could be achieved.

A cold chill went through Nick's whole body as he thought of that purpose.

The Dealer would be at Bern to do the thing he was best at—kill.

But who?

Another chill and, this time, a sip of wine to calm it.

The Dealer planned to assassinate the President and the Vice President of the United States.

How?

By natural causes. Nothing else would be acceptable. Some virus, no doubt. By whom? Under what other scenario would you ever have the President of the United States and the Russian Death Dealer in the same room together?

And without a President and Vice President, who was next in the line of succession?

The Speaker of the House.

Ganicek had stepped aside from the Bern conference. The Vice President had stepped in; and someone else had also stepped in.

And in two days' time, if the Dealer were successful, Ganicek would step up. And so would that someone else.

If the plot were successful, the balance of the relationship between the two super powers would stabilize. And the Premier would take the credit. His Politburo adversaries who had accompanied him to the conference would be removed or silenced.

And the Dealer would stand behind the Premier, with the iron fist of worldwide public opinion at the man's throat.

In Nick's mind there was only one half of a single question left. How was the Dealer going to gain ultimate power over his former boss, who was now Premier of Russia?

It had something to do with the diaries—the diaries that Nick was about to get.

Another movement across the street caught Nick's attention.

A woman, fiftyish and fat, waddled into the shop. The equally buxom shopkeeper came forward to meet her. They exchanged pleasantries, and then Nick's knuckles whitened around the glass of Riesling.

The shop woman's hand went up to the back wall, to the

slots, to the blue envelope. The envelope slid across the counter and disappeared in a large shopping bag.

Money was exchanged, and the envelope's new owner waddled from the shop.

Zero hour, Nick thought, standing up.

Nick stayed well behind the slower moving woman. For all intents and purposes she was out for an evening stroll, which was probably the truth. Now and then she would stop at a shop window and stare. Twice she had entered and made small purchases.

With every block, they moved farther into the poorer section of Berlin. The houses looked older. Many were not completely rejuvenated from the ravages of war. On the streets the faces and hair became darker, Turkish domestic and blue-collar workers.

Every two blocks or so, Omega would pick up the trail and Nick would make a block's detour, only to replace him again. In so doing, the man making the detour could check to see if the followers were being followed.

They weren't, and as the blocks wore on, Nick wondered if Stefan had made his connection clear to them. It had been two years, he had said, since the Dealer had sent the diaries out and the connection for their pickup had been established.

As he moved, Nick scrutinized every face, every movement.

All ordinary. But then, if his hunch was right, the whole caper would turn out to be very ordinary.

Nick came up short. The sound of the woman's shuffling steps had come to a halt. He squinted, his eyes boring down the ill-lit street until he spotted her. She was standing on the stoop of a narrow, two-story house. The only difference between it and its neighbors was a little more paint on the shutters and other woodwork.

From beneath the unseasonably large coat she wore came a key. The heavy, inlaid door swung open and she moved inside.

Almost at the same moment, Omega's blonde head appeared at Nick's shoulder. "I thought the fat old hag would take forever getting here."

"Odd, isn't it—an old Polish woman living in a run-down Turkish neighborhood."

Omega only shrugged.

In the darkness, Nick smiled.

"Check the back for a way in. I'll wait here."

The man faded away on silent feet. In minutes he was back. "There is an alley in the rear—access through a window. I have already jimmied it."

"All right," Nick said. "I'll get her to the front. Once you get in, stay put! We don't want anything burned or shredded before we can get to it, and we don't know who else is in there."

He nodded and disappeared again. Nick counted to one hundred slowly and then made his way down the street. At the door he paused, looking for a nameplate. At last he spotted it, a small brass plate above the door molding, badly in need of polishing: HANS GRUBNER.

He knocked.

"*Ja?*" She was still in her coat.

"*Sprechen sie Deutsch?*"

"*Ja.*"

"*Ist Herr Frommel zu Hause?*"

"*Nein. Herr Frommel ist nicht hier—*"

She barely got the last word out before Nick was through the door, kicking it shut behind him. As gently as possible, he pinned her shoulders to the wall and leaned his face close to hers.

"Cooperate, old woman, and you won't be hurt. Where is the man?"

"What man? I don't—" Her face was white with fear, but there was determination in her jaw and flashing eyes.

"You pick up things, like envelopes, old woman, and you take them to the one they are addressed to. The name on the envelope in your pocket is The Caretaker. Where is the Caretaker?"

"I don't know. . . ."

Nick guessed that the old woman was only a house-keeper and knew very little about what was going on. If he, Nick Carter, knew the whole story, he could have afforded to be a little more gentle and take a little more time.

That was impossible.

He flexed his arm, and instantly the point of his stiletto was against the woman's throat.

"*Where*, old woman!"

She motioned up the stairs just as Omega appeared in the hall. "Is he alone?" Nick barked.

She nodded, and Nick turned to the blonde man. "Tie her up. But that's all, understand?"

He nodded and, Wilhelmina in hand, Nick made for the stairs. Over his shoulder he spotted Omega already tying the woman up with the belt from her own coat.

At the top of the stairs was a long, narrow hall. Light came from under just one of the four doors along it.

"Olga, is that you?"

Nick didn't hesitate. He turned the knob. The door flew open and he darted inside, Wilhelmina ready and cocked.

There was little need for caution. In a rocker beside a low kindled fire sat a very old, white-haired man. Old-fashioned wire-rimmed spectacles perched on the end of his nose, and his lap was encased in a robe. Sitting in the middle of his lap was a thick sheaf of papers between two cheap covers. The whole was tightly bound with string.

"Herr Grubner?"

The old man nodded and tapped the bundle on his lap. "There is no need for the gun. This is what you have come for. I have no means of protecting it. Just tell me of my son."

Nick's brows furrowed. "Your son . . .?"

The man nodded. "I beg of you, whether you come from Stefan or not, just tell me if he is well, if he is alive. When the ad appeared, I hoped—"

"Stefan Borczak is your son?" Nick hissed, pieces falling into place.

"Yes, I—"

It was the last thing the man said. Through the open door beside Nick there was the popping sound made by a silenced revolver. A small, very neat hole appeared in the center of the old man's head. There was only a single drop of blood, and he didn't move.

Nick didn't wait for his turn. He stepped farther to the side and swung the door with all his might. It hit the revolver's long, silenced muzzle first, and then smashed into Omega's face.

The gun flew out of his hand and his body slammed back against the jamb with a crunching sound.

But the big blonde was far from out. His hands flattened before his face, and he came at Nick like a coiled panther. The guy was fast and he knew what he was doing. He also had more guts than brains. Nick could have dropped him with one squeeze of Wilhelmina's trigger, but that didn't deter him.

Nick avoided the first slashing blow by rolling to the wall. The second sheared his ear but left no more damage than the Bells of St. Mary's in his head. The wall beside his head didn't fare as well. Omega's chopping hand went through plaster and lathing like butter.

When Nick saw the damage to the wall and the speed of the recovery after the chop, he knew he couldn't avoid the big blonde killer much longer.

When Omega recoiled and came again, Nick leveled Wilhelmina and squeezed off one shot.

The slug hit him dead center in the right shoulder. It spun his around, and before he could recover, Nick had wrapped his right arm around his neck. He squeezed until the point of Omega's chin was cradled in his elbow. Then, using his own left elbow as a fulcrum off his right hand, he placed his left palm forward at the back of the blonde's head.

"You're the Dealer's man," Nick hissed in his ear. "I knew it almost from the beginning. Too many good men turned down too high-paying a contract, and all of them, to a man, recommended you."

Omega only grunted and struggled to free himself. Nick had to give him credit. The pain had to be excruciating, and he was bleeding like a butchered pig, but he wasn't giving up. Nick tightened his arm and placed a knee in the center of his back.

Quiet, at least for a few seconds, and then groaning with pain.

"It became obvious as well when you shot that Moroccan in Paris. I saw the look on his face just before you blew him away. It didn't hit me until later, but it was a look of recognition."

More struggling, but no words.

"What was the scenario for tonight? Was the old man supposed to die or was that a last-minute ad-lib? Was I supposed to buy it too, or was the old man going to be another accident like the Moroccan?"

"Fuck you," came the half-throttled reply.

"No, you blood thirsty bastard, fuck you."

Nick stiffened the knee in his back, lifted, and twisted the man's head between his two powerful arms.

He heard the snap, felt the body go limp, and dropped it.

Quickly he stepped over Omega to the old man.

Damn, Nick thought, lifting the entwined sheaf of papers from the old man's lap, the one thing I never dreamed of. Stefan sent the Death Dealer's private papers to his own father for safekeeping!

Downstairs, Nick located the old woman in the hall closet. Omega had tied her up, all right. He had also slit her throat.

And it isn't the end yet, Nick thought. But hopefully there will only be one more.

CHAPTER ELEVEN

Nick slipped through the back door of the pension. There was a narrow stairway vaguely illuminated by a five-watt bulb. As he climbed, he felt the strain and weariness seep through his bones.

But he couldn't rest—not yet.

His and Hela's rooms were on the fifth floor. Nick stopped at the third. There were only four rooms fore and aft. He tapped on 3-A.

"Yes?"

"It's me, Carter."

The door opened quickly and a young, intense man with bright blue eyes and the body of a fullback stepped aside to let Nick enter.

His name was Eric Hawn. He was attached to Nick on special duty from the German Federal Intelligence Service—the Bundesnachtendienst, or, more simply, the BND. Right now he was in well-worn jeans and a blue work shirt. If anyone looked closely, all they would see was a clean-cut young man who probably worked in a factory or garage somewhere.

In actual fact, Eric was highly trained by the American

CIA and more than capable of handling anything Nick had to throw at him. Up until now it hadn't been much more than surveillance.

Nick hoped it would amount to only that, surveillance.

"Got a drink—anything."

Hawn gestured to a bare round table beneath the room's only light. "Just schnapps—sorry."

"S'fine. What've ya got?"

While the man flipped open a small notebook and spoke very efficiently in short, clipped tones, Nick poured a shot of the clear liquid, downed it, and quickly poured a second.

"Just as you said she would, the subject—"

"Woman."

"The woman went through your room right after you left. From the amount of time it took her, I would say she did it very thoroughly."

Nick nodded after the downing of the second drink. It would take her a while to find the file, he thought, pouring yet a third shot of the smooth potion. He had hidden the file well. His guess was that it would take even someone with Hela's experience at least a half hour to find it.

"Go on," he said.

"She walked to the toll booth at the corner and made two calls—neither of them long enough to trace. Approximately an hour later she sent down for the innkeeper's son. Told the old man she wanted the boy to run an errand for her."

"And . . ." Nick said, slumping onto one of the table's two chairs.

"She gave the boy ten Deutsche marks to deliver a package to an office suite in the Europa-Center. It was the offices of Komendiest Imports. We know it as a front for East German activities."

Nick nodded. "Figures. Could you trace it from there?"

Hawn nodded. "Luckily we have a man—rather, a

woman, actually—on the inside there. It went directly and express to Lufthansa Air Freight at Tegel Airport.''

"Destination?"

"München."

Again Nick nodded and ground his thumbs into burning eyes. "Any further activity?"

"*Ja*—I mean, yes. She has asked at the desk three times for messages."

"She would," Nick growled, thinking of Omega's face grotesquely contorted in death at his feet.

"That's about it," Eric said, snapping the notebook shut.

"Not quite." Nick tossed him the bundle. "Have your boys scrawl a bunch of weird cyphers on about as many pages as this to make a new package almost as thick. Then bind it back up with the same wrappings. Will it take long?"

"Shouldn't. They're downstairs in the truck."

"Good," Nick said. "And on your way back, check with your office medical team and see if the hypo arrived from London."

"Don't have to," Hawn replied, producing a small leather case from his bag. "It's already here."

Nick flipped the lid on the case to reveal a hypodermic needle, syringe, and two ampules of what he hoped was a surefire antidote to plague.

New bundle in hand, Nick paused before her door and listened. He could hear faint movement, like pacing, beyond the door.

He rapped twice with a single knuckle, paused, and rapped again. He knew it was only his imagination, but he was sure he heard a gasp of surprise seep through the thin wood panel.

"Nick . . .?"

"You expecting someone else?"

There was a moment's pause. Just long enough, Nick

thought, for her to compose herself.

The chain rattled, the lock turned, and the door opened wide.

She stood calm, cool and composed in a traveling suit of some tweedy material. Beneath the jacket, a flouncy white silk blouse went all the way to her neck and disguised the marvelous contours of her breasts.

At the moment, Hela was far from on the make.

"Nick—thank God."

She came into his arms, throwing her own around his neck. Her scent filled his nostrils and her body felt soft and warm. Over her shoulder he saw her two bags sitting neatly in the center of the room.

"You're efficient."

"What?" No alarm in her voice, and only a slight tic at the corner of one eye when she backed off to face him.

Nick nodded his head toward the luggage. "You're packed, you're dressed, you're ready to roll."

"Oh, yes." She didn't stumble, but the pause said a lot. "I know we weren't scheduled to leave for Bern until morning, but I thought I'd be ready tonight just in case your plans changed."

"My plans?"

She shrugged as he moved by her into the room. "I thought if everything went all right, you might want to leave early."

"Yeah, you're right—I might have." He slumped wearily into an overstuffed chair and made a point of dropping the twine-covered sheaf of papers on the coffee table beside him. "But as beat as I am now, all I can think of is sleep."

It took all the willpower she could muster not to glue her eyes to the papers. As it was, she let them stray twice, and Nick could sense how hard it was for her to return her gaze to his.

"Is that . . .?"

Nick nodded. "The very same; the Dealer's famous diaries, and they're bloody as hell."

"What?"

"The old man who had them, his housekeeper, and the guy I hired to set up the hit—all dead."

"You . . .?"

"Just one of them. The guy I hired. He turned out to be a double, the Dealer's man. I shot him and then broke his neck."

"He's dead?" she said.

"Very." Her reaction had been tense to that point. Now, even though it was barely perceptible, Nick could see her calm. "Got anything to drink in your bag?"

"No."

Nick tossed her his room key. "There's a pint of Scotch in a leather case on the bureau in my room—mind?"

"Of course not."

She moved through the door. Nick traced her movements by sound as he lit the last cigarette in his pack. The smoke burned deeply in his lungs, the pain of it momentarily jolting away the weariness in his body.

Hela returned with the flask and two glasses already poured. Their hands touched briefly when she handed him one of the tumblers. Lightly, Nick ran one of his fingers down one of hers to the nail. He noted the clear polish and felt the almost honed edge with his fingertip.

"How do you manage to play with nails so long?" he asked idly.

She laughed low in her throat. "I told you, I rarely play anymore."

"Yeah, you did. I forgot."

She sat down opposite him, and Nick sipped his Scotch. Over the rim of his glass he studied her, as she had once studied him.

"I guess it's over now," she said, "except for Bern."

"Yeah, I've pretty well figured it all out now. Whoever

the Dealer is, we should be able to nip his empire-building in the bud.''

''Empire-building?''

Nick leaned back in the chair. Massaging his temples with his free hand, he slitted his eyes and let his voice fade into a somnambulist monotone.

''The Dealer is a futuristic thinking man. My guess is that every plot he made, every life he took, every idea he conceived from the beginning of his career, had one solitary purpose.''

''Which was?''

''He wanted a way to control the governments of both super powers.''

Her laugh was guttural. ''That's impossible. Such a thing is inconceivable!''

''To the normal mind, perhaps. But the Dealer's mind isn't normal, and his ambitions are astronomical.''

Nick continued to speak in a low, even voice, telling her what he suspected she already knew.

He told her of the mole, Jacek, working for Ganicek, but not knowing that Ganicek himself was a mole working for the Dealer, planted years before to become, one day, the President of the United States.

There was an appropriate wide-eyed gasp from Hela, and she quickly refilled their glasses.

''Jacek's sole purpose was to kill the Speaker of the House and elevate Ganicek to that position. One thing went awry in the Dealer's plan. Jacek got a conscience. He was going to be killed anyway, but the timetable had to be stepped up. But the Dealer even used that to his advantage. He killed Jacek and then planted the evidence of Russian malfeasance in a suitcase in the man's car.''

''But why would the Dealer—a Russian—give away Soviet secrets?''

''Because at the Bern conference he wanted a stalemate between the two countries, an equal power in each fist. You see, Hela, the Dealer is going to kill the President and the Vice President at Bern. Normally that would have many complications. But not if they were killed by a strange untraceable disease that had already killed several people.''

''Our people—''

''That's right. The Dealer's man, Ganicek, steps into the Presidency. One super power controlled!''

''And the other?''

Nick rested his hand on the bound papers. ''The Dealer would control the Premier with these. This could blow the lid off Soviet crimes, going all the way back to Stalin. Published, the whole world would revolt against Mother Russia.''

''But what would be the use of such power? What would the Dealer hope to gain?''

Nick shrugged. ''More power. As silly as it sounds, I think the Dealer's ego is such that his only aspiration is to be the most powerful man on earth. It's not so rare— Hitler, Charlemagne, Napoleon—they all had the same ego.''

''That's amazing.''

''Yeah, it is,'' Nick said, heaving himself to his feet. ''But now that we know who Ganicek really is, and the fact that we have the diaries, it shouldn't be too difficult to stop him at Bern.

''No,'' Hela said, her eyes flickering over the tied bundle as Nick picked it up, ''it shouldn't.''

''I'm going to grab a shower and get some rest. We'll leave in the morning. There's no rush now.''

Nick left her, glass in hand, staring at the coffee table, at the spot where the papers had been sitting.

For almost a half hour, Nick stood beneath the steaming spray of the shower head, relaxing, soaping himself. When he finally emerged, drying himself with a large, fluffy European towel, she was lying across the bed.

''Since we're not leaving until morning,'' she said, tossing her hair away from her forehead, ''I thought we might as well make use of the night.''

She looked up. She was cool, every inch the voluptuous siren as her dark eyes locked onto his gaze, issuing their own kind of challenge.

Nick smiled, and she smiled in return. ''I don't know if I'm up to it,'' he said.

''All men, Nick, are up to it with the right provocation.'' She only moved slightly, but it was enough to make her bare breasts dance, to make her hips and thighs evoke desire.

Nick dropped the towel and eased himself onto the bed. She moved against him, all warmth, all steaming woman, all Cheshire cat with the smile on her sensual lips.

''You are a marvelous lover, Nick. Make me a woman who can accept love. I told you it would be better in Berlin.''

''Yes, you did.''

He kissed her, letting his tongue run along her lips and then delve into her waiting, warm mouth. Her breast was warm in his hand, firm yet soft at the same time. Her thighs captured one of his legs and she began to move against him.

His lips moved over her ear and down her throat to her shoulder. He felt her hand slide up his side, her nails tickling his flesh.

''Love me, Nick, hurt me! Not too much, just a little— like this.''

He felt the nails start to bite into his buttocks. As casually as he could, Nick captured the hand before its deadly talons could break the flesh.

He knew he wouldn't be able to take this all the way, to actually make love to her. But he had managed enough foreplay to make it convincing.

''It's going to be quite an ego trip for me,'' he growled, bringing her hand up to his lips. ''Beating the Dealer, watching him die.''

"Forget the Dealer, Nick—at least for a while. It's just the two of us now."

Nick kissed the back of her hand and let his lips trail down her fingers. His eyes moved ahead to her nails.

She had redone them before coming to his room.

The polish on them before had been clear. Now it was blood red.

"You redid your nails."

"Of course," she replied, trying to make the withdrawing of her hand from his as casual as possible. "I wanted to be beautiful for you. I combed my hair and put on perfume as well." She couldn't hide the nervous sound in the laughter that followed her words.

"Jacek was killed by a puncture wound. The Speaker by a pinprick when he ignited a lighter. The two on the plane contracted their 'virus' from a tiny prick to their wrists, so small they weren't detected in the first autopsy."

"What are you getting at?" Hela's voice was cold now, all traces of lusty desire extinguished by swift-moving thoughts.

"The poet—Janusz—"

"What about him?"

Nick didn't have to feel the tenseness in her body. He could sense it. The feminine, yet athletically hardened muscles in her arms and legs, began to bunch. The cords in her neck began to rise, and her whole body began to coil.

"There were scratches on Janusz's back, all up and down its entire length including his buttocks. They were scratches made by a woman in the throes of passion—the kind of scratches a man would welcome if they told him he was satisfying a woman's needs. They were deep, gouging scratches, from nails much like these. . . ."

Nick reached for her wrists, but they weren't there for him to capture.

In an instant she was on him, clawing like a cat. The long, deadly talons of her nails went for his eyes, his flesh, anywhere they could make contact and dig in. At the same time, she swung her body around so she could bring her knee up into his groin.

Nick blocked her knee with his hip and managed to grab both of her wrists at last.

"It's over, Hela, the charade is over. I know who the Dealer is, and I know who you are. I'm going to kill him. Don't make me kill you as well."

Her only reply was a near maniacal laugh.

Hela struggled like a hellcat, with more power and energy than he would have thought possible. She managed to free one arm and lashed forward, her hand like a claw. The nails went directly for his eyes. She missed his eyes, but Nick could feel the pain and then warm blood as she slashed his forehead. Another swipe, as quick as a serpent, and all five of the deadly talons had opened his cheek.

He swung his own free arm in a wide arc and landed a solid blow to the side of her head. She sprawled, cursing, off the bed and across the floor.

A blow of that force would have felled most men, but not Hela. She was on her knees by the time Nick reached her. He managed to regain her wrists, but just as he did, she twisted, taking them both to the floor.

Together they rolled, Nick panting now and holding on as best he could, Hela using everything—her teeth, her feet, her knees—but most of all, trying to free her wrists and bring those nails back into play.

Her face came up close to his as Nick regained his feet and pulled her up along with him. Her eyes were bright but coldly vacant. There was no anger, no love, no hate, literally no emotion in her eyes or her features.

She, like Nick himself, was only a machine.

And then it started. The fingers gripping her wrists

began to grow numb. A slight mist began to form over his eyes, and he felt contractions in his chest.

"You're dying, Carter," Hela hissed in his ear. "You're dying on your feet. Keep struggling—it makes the blood flow faster, shoots it right to your heart."

Like her eyes and her features, there was no emotion in her voice.

Nick staggered against her. His legs had suddenly stopped working. He felt a cold sweat oozing from his pores, and his chest felt as though it was between the two tongues of a vise.

He hadn't even realized that he had dropped his hold on her wrists. But there they were, her hands dancing before his eyes. One of them insolently smashed against his face, sending him sprawling across the bed on his back.

She was on him in an instant, the hands poised over him, curled into claws. And then she struck, all ten nails finding the soft part of his belly. The fingers curled and drove the blood-red spikes as far as they could into his gut.

Satisfied, she moved away from him. For several minutes she stood, statuelike, staring down at him. She watched his face flush, and listened intently as the wracking cough became a wheezing rattle.

When he was deathly still, she went to the bath. Nick lay watching her through slitted eyes. It was as if he were floating, watching her in slow motion as she washed her hands and methodically brushed her hair. Dreamlike, she applied fresh makeup and returned to the bedroom to dress.

Nick didn't move. He couldn't. His mind was still alive, but his body felt numb and dead.

Fully dressed, with the sheaf of papers under her arm, Hela paused in the doorway and stared back at him.

Odd, he thought, now she smiles.

And then she was gone.

Go, baby, Nick thought, run to him. Take him

Borczak's precious, bloody diaries and tell him everything is fine. Tell him Carter's dead. Tell him the road is clear to make his bloody deal. Make him think that no one knows!

The minutes dragged by. Nick kept mental count. At the end of an hour, there was still no movement. Another half hour, and he began to sweat.

Jesus, he thought, sensing rather than feeling the sweat pour off him, the hypo is worthless—the antidote isn't going to work!

And then, just over two hours later, he began to feel the numbness subside.

Shortly after that he felt his first movement; his lips curled into a smile.

CHAPTER TWELVE

The sigh that slipped around Hawk's cigar was one of contentment. His eyes flicked up from the paper-strewn desk to where Nick sat slouched down in an overstuffed chair.

"This stuff is dynamite."

"I figured it would be. The real Stefan Borczak lived on hate. This was his form of revenge."

Hawk chuckled. "And it might have all worked."

"It probably would have worked, long enough anyway, if Omega had killed the old man before he admitted that he was Stefan's father. Or if Omega had been able to kill me, as he was supposed to, and get the real diaries to the Dealer."

"The President has had two very private and very secret conferences with the Premier already this afternoon."

"And . . .?" Nick asked.

"The Russians want to cooperate all the way," Hawk replied, and swept his hand over the papers. "They want all this kept quiet. They'll deal any way they can to get it all back and all hushed up."

Nick felt tenseness crawl up his spine. "You mean we'd give it back to them?"

Hawk shrugged. "It's part of the game, Nick, you know that. They give us the considerations we want, we give them their life back. Besides, we could never release this stuff, and they know it. It would be like a nuclear strike if we did. And before the repercussions hit, they would be forced to retaliate."

Nick groaned but nodded. He knew all too well it was part of the game. "What about the Dealer?"

Hawk paused, letting his eyes stray from Carter's. "The Russians want him back."

"What for?"

"Probably to find out what other little bombs he's got planted around the world."

"And we want to keep him for the same reason," Nick said with disgust.

Hawk heaved his big frame from the desk chair and moved to a high, arched window that looked toward the Alps. He stood in silence for several moments, with his hands entwined behind his back and his head veiled in a cloud of smoke. "Not necessarily," he said finally. "The Dealer is as awkward in our hands as he is in theirs. The President didn't tell the Premier everything, but enough to make the old boy sweat."

"Where is he now?"

"The Dealer?"

"Who else?" Nick replied.

"Up there," Hawk gestured toward the mountains, "in a chalet. Your friend Anatole and five of our best are guarding him."

"And he doesn't know that it's over?"

"No, not yet. But he will tomorrow, when the conference starts and he's not there."

Nick let his mind work, trying to interpret Hawk's thoughts as well as his words. "So when he does find out that we know, and that we have the real diaries, he could get word out somehow and still raise hell.''

Hawk nodded. ''That's why your deception with Hela was a masterpiece. She delivered the mock package you provided and took off. The Dealer believes they're the real thing, so he's been quiet.''

''And the woman?''

''He told her to disappear until it was over. On the scene, she might be dangerous if we suspected her of killing you. You are dead, you know, as far as he's concerned.''

''That was the idea,'' Nick said, moving across the room to stand at Hawk's side. ''Now, how do we use the advantage?''

''We nailed the woman before she left Vienna to cross the river into Hungary. She injected herself before we could stop her. I think when we come down on Ganicek, he'll do the same.''

''Hopefully,'' Nick murmured.

Hawk gave a barely perceptible nod and echoed the word, ''Hopefully.''

''So there's only the Dealer himself,'' Nick intoned. ''As long as he's alive, even in custody, here or over there, he's still got worldwide contacts known only to himself, and loyal only to him.''

''That's right,'' Hawk said, another cloud of smoke obscuring his features. ''As long as he's alive . . .''

The words trailed off. Neither Hawk nor Nick's head turned. Both men stared straight ahead, to the lights of a chalet on the far mountain.

At last Nick spoke again. ''You'll inform Anatole so he can get everything ready?''

''I will.''

The chalet was easily accessible from the rear by climbing over huge stones in the snow. For Nick it would have been easily accessible from the front, but the Dealer had insisted on occupying a front room. From there he could monitor everyone who came and went.

Nick didn't want to announce his arrival just yet.

One by one he stepped over the stones until he reached a low, Romanesque balustrade that encircled the rear courtyard of the chalet. Easily he vaulted the balustrade and then walked casually across the courtyard.

Ahead of him, one of the tall, multi-paned French doors opened and Anatole stepped out.

"Good evening, my friend."

"Anatole." Together they stepped into the high-ceiling room. "Where is he?"

"In his room. He has been there all evening."

"He suspects nothing?"

"Nothing, as far as I can tell. And he hasn't tried to communicate with the outside."

Nick nodded. "You are alone?"

"The others left a half hour ago, the same way you arrived. There is a key in the gray Bentley out front for your departure."

"Servants?"

"Off for tonight. I dismissed them the moment word came up from Hawk."

Nick held out his hand. "Goodbye, my friend. Go back to your boat and forget all this."

"Have I ever remembered all the other times, heh?"

" 'Til the next time."

Anatole sighed. "For me, I think there will be no next time. This time my age is beginning to tell on me. Everything that is necessary has been planted. All you need do is connect the two loose wires in the electrical box near the front door."

Nick nodded, and without another word Anatole crossed the courtyard. Nick watched until his figure was swallowed in darkness and then turned and mounted the wide stairway to the second floor.

"A moment please," was the reply to Nick's knock.

Nick didn't wait. He pushed open the door and walked into the room. Stefan Borczak was turned away from him, his hands working at his face.

"There's no need," Nick said. "It's over. You can leave them out."

The man tensed, his shoulders hunched. After a moment's hesitation, he turned. His hands dropped to his chest. In one of them was a gray opaque eyeglass, the kind used by film actors to give the aura of sightlessness to their eyes for close-ups when they are portraying a blind person. Its mate was in the man's left eye. His right eye was blue, brightly blue, and gleaming at Nick.

Nick had no trouble remembering where he had seen that gleaming eye, and its mate, before. In fact, if the room was a bit darker, he could almost imagine the both of them back in Berlin, by the wall, those eyes looking up at him out of the shadows caused by the brim of a slouched hat.

"Your people found an antidote."

Nick nodded. "It was fairly simple once we broke the virus down into its components."

"And how did you know that I and Stefan Borczak were one in the same?"

"It clicked when the old man in Berlin told me his real name."

"A pity Gerhard couldn't silence him before he spoke, and, of course, an equal pity he couldn't silence you as well. I commend you, Carter. Gerhard, the one you called Omega, was the very best."

"Not as good as you and I," Nick said, letting a disarming smile play across his face.

"That's true—obviously."

He dropped the eyeglass he held to the table in front of him. Then he moved his hands back to his face and removed the other. When he looked up again, Nick felt cold sweat cover his body.

There was pure evil in the man's eyes, made even more evil by what Nick saw as a touch of madness.

"Did you kill the real Stefan?" Nick asked.

"Yes, the moment I found out what he was doing. I would have killed him eventually anyway. His identity was always the one I planned to use to come over."

"You cremated the body?"

"Of course."

"And then it took you four years to find out where Stefan had sent the information he had accumulated."

The Dealer nodded. "I knew his father had defected years before and Stefan was to join him. I wrongly supposed that Stefan would contact his old friend, Jacek, and tell him where the diaries were. I gave him every opportunity."

"But he didn't."

"No. So I had to find them myself."

Nick pulled the narrow-cylindered, specially designed pistol from his pocket and checked the load as he spoke. "Why didn't you just have Omega get them on his own?"

"Safety. In case the old man made a copy. I knew, with your credentials, he would tell you." The Dealer paused and, taking up his cane, moved to a desk where he had obviously been working. "I suppose this is a copy of the real thing."

"It is," Nick replied.

"I thought so. The cypher is childish and makes no sense—far beneath what I have expected of Stefan."

"Did you really think you could get away with it?" Nick growled.

The Dealer turned and started to walk slowly across the room toward Nick. "Absolutely. By the way, how do you plan on eliminating me?"

"With this," Nick said.

He raised the gun and fired. The stiletto-thin dart hit the Dealer in the right thigh. It penetrated the thigh muscle about three inches, leaving two inches of slender steel protruding from the man's leg.

The Dealer stopped and looked down at his leg without a sign of emotion. Then he looked back up at Nick.

"The virus?" Nick nodded. "Amazing. I didn't think you could work up the formula that quickly. But since you did, you can join me."

In an instant the limp disappeared as the man flew toward Nick. As he lunged, the cane flipped in his hand and the gold head sailed directly toward Nick's chest.

Nick was ready. At the last second, he dropped to his knees and reached up to grasp the cane with both hands. At the same time, he brought his shoulder up under the man's gut with all the spring in his legs.

Dropping the cane behind him, Nick chopped twice at the back of the Dealer's neck. He went down, groggy, but not out.

No matter.

Nick secured his feet quickly with his own belt and then his hands with a sash he ripped from the curtains. Then he retrieved the cane and bent over the Dealer, rolling the man to his back.

"About the virus?"

"Yes."

"You're right, we couldn't break down the formula that fast. At least not enough to reproduce it."

Nick easily located the protruding needle in the gold head of the cane. The Dealer actually smiled as Nick pressed it into the fleshy part of his thigh.

Sixty seconds later, Nick dropped the cane and leaned back on his haunches to light a cigarette.

"Drag?" he asked, extending the cigarette to the man.

"No, I've never used them."

"Yeah," Nick hissed, "they will kill you, in time."

"Speaking of time, it takes about three to five minutes."

"I know," Nick said, exhaling. "Remember?"

"Ah, yes." A pause. "Hela?"

"Dead. She injected herself."

The Dealer smiled again. "Good girl."

Nick sat smoking as he watched the sweats begin.

"Who are you, or were you, really?" he asked at last.

"Would it really matter if you knew?" replied the now raspy voice.

"No, not really."

Five minutes later, it was over. Nick checked the pulse twice to make sure, and then made his way downstairs to the switchbox. He connected the wires and went on out to the Bentley.

The powerful engine started at once. Nick eased the car into gear and drove through the estate's front gate. He turned toward the road leading up to the mountain. He had reached a rise above the chateau when the first explosion raised hell with the peaceful Swiss countryside. By the time he had stopped the car, four more had rocked the air and the chalet directly below him was engulfed in flames.

He waited until there was nothing but a huge ball of flame, denoting that nothing inside would ever be identified, and then began idling down the mountain.

When he hit a straightaway, he pulled a fresh pack of cigarettes from his pocket and unwrapped it.

He paused when the lighter was halfway to the tip, but only for an instant.

As the harsh Turkish smoke filled his lungs, he thought that at least they were a slow death.

DON'T MISS THE NEXT NEW NICK CARTER SPY THRILLER

THE ISTANBUL DECISION

Whether it was the reasonableness of the man's tone that convinced them or the familiar bulge in his trench coat pocket, it was impossible to say. But the three turned and without a further word walked up the hall in the direction from which they'd come, leaving Carter alone in the corridor. A moment later the lights went out, plunging the corridor into darkness with only a small amount of light coming from the end doors.

He waited a few seconds to make sure they'd really gone, then began moving again, cautiously but quickly, in the direction of Judit Konya's apartment. The speed with which Kobelev's man had intercepted the two in the hall was disturbing. Obviously, they were not only barring people from entering the building, but were keeping a close watch on the interior as well, probably through the small chicken-wired windows at either end of the hall.

He pushed along, his back against the wall, until he

reached what he considered to be the most likely door. There was no name on it, nothing to distinguish it from any other door facing the hall, except it was situated where he thought her apartment should be. There were small marks along the bottom of the jamb, the kind made by the knock of the steel footrests of a wheelchair when it's not turned short enough.

The door was unlocked. He came through, low and to one side, the Luger in both hands trained on two figures on the other side of the very dark room. One faced him in an old-fashioned wicker wheelchair. She was a noble-looking woman with features seemingly etched from stone. Her eyes were closed and her head held at an attentive angle as though she were listening, although what she was listening to was not clear, except that it was not in this room, or perhaps even in this world. On the wall behind her and to one side hung a crucifix done in the old Polish style. Myriad votive candles flickered on the table before it, providing what little light there was.

The other kneeled in front of her as though praying, the houndstooth coat stretched across his broad back and over the collar was a thatch of snow-white hair. Kobelev!

Nick fired twice, the shots slamming Kobelev forward and to the left. The old woman's eyes sprang open, the knuckle of her left index finger to her mouth.

Carter stood slowly and came toward her, keeping the gun on the body sprawled headlong on the floor. There had been something very peculiar about the way it fell.

He rolled it over with the toe of his shoe. The face was a blank, pink cloth stitched in the general proportions of the human countenance. Fleetingly, he wondered where the dummy had come from. They certainly hadn't brought it in from the limo.

A noise forced him to turn around. It was one of those sounds that chill the blood several degrees without ever fully registering in the brain, like the rattle of a snake underfoot, or the roar of an engine that's too close for comfort. Only in this case it was more muted, the simple metal-on-metal as a hammer is drawn back and a cylinder clicked into position.

—From THE ISTANBUL DECISION
A New Nick Carter Spy Thriller
From Charter in September

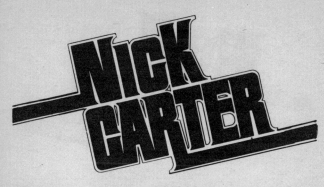

☐	14172-2	**THE DEATH STAR AFFAIR**	$2.50
☐	14169-2	**DEATHLIGHT**	$2.50
☐	15244-9	**THE DOMINICAN AFFAIR**	$2.50
☐	17014-5	**THE DUBROVNIK MASSACRE**	$2.25
☐*	63176-3	**THE PARISIAN AFFAIR**	$2.50
☐*	67081-4	**PLEASURE ISLAND**	$2.50
☐	71133-2	**THE REDOLMO AFFAIR**	$1.95
☐	14217-6	**THE DEATH DEALER**	$2.50
☐	95305-0	**THE YUKON TARGET**	$2.50
☐	42781-2	**THE KALI DEATH CULT**	$2.50
☐	71228-2	**REICH FOUR**	$1.95

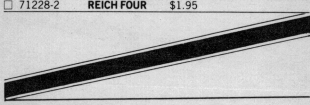

Available at your local bookstore or return this form to:

 CHARTER BOOKS
Book Mailing Service
P.O. Box 690, Rockville Centre, NY 11571

Please send me the titles checked above. I enclose _____
Include $1.00 for postage and handling if one book is ordered; 50¢ per book for
two or more. California, Illinois, New York and Tennessee residents please add
sales tax. (allow six weeks for delivery)

NAME _____

ADDRESS _____

CITY _____ STATE/ZIP _____

A8

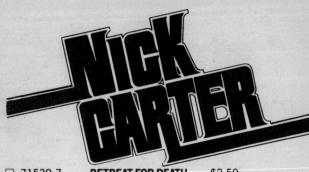

NICK CARTER

☐ 71539-7	**RETREAT FOR DEATH**	$2.50	
☐ 75035-4	**THE SATAN TRAP**	$1.95	
☐ 76347-2	**THE SIGN OF THE COBRA**	$2.25	
☐ 77193-9	**THE SNAKE FLAG CONSPIRACY**		$2.25
☐ 77413-X	**SOLAR MENACE**	$2.50	
☐ 79073-9	**THE STRONTIUM CODE**	$2.50	
☐ 79077-1	**THE SUICIDE SEAT**	$2.25	
☐ 81025-X	**TIME CLOCK OF DEATH**	$1.75	
☐ 82348-3	**THE TREASON GAME**	$2.50	
☐ 82407-2	**TRIPLE CROSS**	$1.95	
☐ 82726-8	**TURKISH BLOODBATH**	$2.25	
☐ 87192-5	**WAR FROM THE CLOUDS**	$2.25	

Available at your local bookstore or return this form to:

 CHARTER BOOKS
Book Mailing Service
P.O. Box 690, Rockville Centre, NY 11571

Please send me the titles checked above. I enclose _____
Include $1.00 for postage and handling if one book is ordered; 50¢ per book for
two or more. California, Illinois, New York and Tennessee residents please add
sales tax.

NAME _____

ADDRESS _____

CITY _____ STATE/ZIP _____

(allow six weeks for delivery)   **A8**